DRAGON'S HOPE

RED PLANET DRAGONS OF TAJSS BOOK 4

MIRANDA MARTIN

CONTENTS

Before the generation ship crashed on this desert alien planet I was a Vagrant. Unplanned and unwanted, struggling to survive.

Now we're on Tajss and if not for the natives, seven foot tall dragon-men with wings and tails and scales, we'd all be dead.

My new friends are all finding love and I couldn't be happier for them. I want to fit in, I want to have a place and a purpose, and strangely enough the only one who might understand is one of those scaled dragon-men.

I wanted comfort and attention but it turns out 'one night stand' doesn't translate into Zmaj. He wants more and won't give up until he claims his treasure. Me.

Dragon's Hope is a full length scifi novel with a happily ever after ending, plenty of steam, bloody battles and alien-human intrigue. It is standalone and co-written by Miranda Martin and one of the hottest science fiction romance authors out there, Juno Wells.

DRAGON'S HOPE is BOOK 4 of the <u>RED PLANET DRAGONS OF TAJSS</u>. *You do not have to read them all in order to understand the plot, but the story will be **much** richer if you do!*

It began with Dragon's Baby and carries on from there!

ASTAROT

*T*wo blazing suns shine high overhead, their heat warming my scales as I stare out across the striated sands. We hunt for Bivo, the large animal that will feed my treasure's people for days.

"Dude, I don't know what you're thinking. Everybody knows Tennant was the best doctor," Cecil says.

The irritating human male's voice breaks my concentration and I let slide back the second protective lids of my eyes and turn.

"You're insane," Bryce replies, rolling his eyes. "Baker's the best, period."

"Oh my God!" Cecil's voice rises to a high, scratchy sound that makes my scales itch. "I don't understand the fascination people have with the original series. The acting is flat and the special effects are terrible."

"How can you not understand that's part of the magic?"

"Magic? That's what that was? I thought it was a bunch of set guys throwing on old tires and other pieces of junk and calling them monsters!" Cecil says, laughing.

"Do you two ever shut up?" Lana asks, looking over her shoulder at them.

She holds the staff I gave her against her shoulder, like I showed her, her eyes flashing brilliantly. My cock stiffens as desire stirs. She's beautiful. My treasure has the lushest of soft curves and dark, beautiful fur on her head. She has yet to realize we are meant to be mates but one day I will claim her.

The two human males look at each other, smile, then return their gazes to Lana.

"No," they say in unison, then laugh.

"I could really learn to hate you," she mutters, turning away.

Bryce punches Cecil in the arm. Cecil grabs his arm rubbing it, glaring at Bryce.

"What was that for?" he asks.

"She was talking to you dumb ass," Bryce says.

"No way, she totally meant you."

"I was talking about both of you," Lana tosses over her shoulder without bothering to turn around.

She and I lead the way further into the vast, red desert. The chatter behind us continues as the two young human males continue their mindless banter.

"Look at her ass," Cecil says.

"What I would do to that," Bryce says.

"Nothing," Cecil laughs. "You couldn't get it up."

Lana sighs and shakes her head. She glances over and I shrug. I do not like the scent of their desire for her, it takes an effort of will to keep back the bijass, that primal and possessive rage waiting to consume any male Zmaj.

"Why did we agree to let them come along?" she asks.

"Gershom insisted," I answer.

"Can't stand him either," she says.

I say nothing to that because I can't disagree. I've never known somebody as off putting as Gershom. He's a hateful human, filled with anger and an obvious drive for power. The chatter of the other two grows distant as Lana and I outpace them. I like being out here. I feel at home. I don't have a place in Drakonov, Ladon's city. The other Zmaj have their mates. If we had a proper society still, there would be dozens of other males like me, unmated, and they would be my companions. But there are no others like me. I am alone and I do not belong.

I spread my wings, shrugging downward for lift so it is easier to get to the top of the dune we are climbing. My tail shifts side to side as I crouch down and close my outer lids so I can see further into the distance. My scales tingle as Lana crouches next to me and my prime penis hardens with her nearness, demanding I claim her as my treasure. Ignoring it, I scan the horizon.

"What do you see?" she asks.

"There," I say, pointing.

"Damn, I can't see it yet," she says, gritting her teeth.

"Bivo," I say. "Large herd, might be ten to fifteen."

"One of them could feed us for a few days," she says.

I nod. Food is our number one problem. Too many of the survivors of the human ship that crashed here are incapable. They can't hunt. They couldn't survive without the handful of us that make everything go right. The supplies they brought with them are dwindling, but Lana is different. Since we first organized these hunting parties she's thrown herself into them with enthusiasm. My treasure is eager to learn and I admire her, doing my best to aid her efforts.

"Yeah," I agree.

"Shit," she says, looking over her shoulder. "What are those two idiots getting into now?"

I follow her gaze and see that the two of them are approaching a small cluster of plants. "They should stay away from that."

Lana rises to her feet. "Hey!" she yells. "You two, Beavis and Butthead, get away from that."

I follow along behind her, ready to help, but more interested in letting them learn a lesson the hard way. Cecil looks over his shoulder and grins, waving her off.

"It's all good," he says, motioning with the knife in his hand.

It's a selagi they're approaching. Like most life on Tajss it's dangerous, but less than many other things. It will not kill the humans but maybe it'll wake them up. Bryce crouches down, reaching out for one of the dried, brown leaves. The selagi appears to looks desiccated but that's part of its disguise. As soon as Bryce touches it, he cries out in pain and surprise. He tries to jump back but the selagi stalk wraps around his arm, holding him in place. The brown, desiccated looking leaves take on a reddish tint as the plant releases its poison onto the skin.

"Holy shit! Help!" Bryce cries.

"Shit man," Cecil says, rushing forward.

Lana looks at me and I shrug. She shakes her head, then sighs. "Damn it."

Holding her staff at the ready she rushes forward and stops just outside the range of the selagi. She swings her bow staff around and slams it down in the middle of the plant. It retreats, pulling down into the loose sand and letting Bryce go. Bryce stumbles backwards and falls onto his ass. Cecil grabs him under his arms and pulls him further away.

Lana stalks towards them, still holding her staff at the ready. I hope she's about to crack one of them over the head with it. I doubt it will make any difference with them but it would make me feel better.

"What were you two idiots thinking?"

"It looked like we could smoke it," Cecil says.

"Are you kidding me?" Lana asks in utter disbelief.

"Sure?" Bryce says, shrugging.

"Everything out here is trying to kill you and all you two want is to get high," Lana says.

"What does 'get high' mean?" I ask.

"It means these two morons want to get into an herbal induced euphoria," Lana responds.

"Ah, they would need koren root for that."

Both human males stare at me with open mouths. "Where do we get that?" Cecil asks.

Lana throws up her hands, "Why on earth do you even want it!"

"You have a little smoke, everybody relaxes, and then things are just easier," Bryce shrugs.

"Yeah, hell, she might even put out if she had a little smoke," Cecil says.

"There's not enough smoke in the world for me to put out for you two," Lana retorts. "We're out here to do a job, do you remember that? You know, feed the survivors. The ones who are counting on us back in the city?"

"Yeah, sure," Bryce says.

"Damn, what a party pooper," Cecil says.

"I swear, if you to do that again I'll crack you over the head myself," Lana says.

"Okay, we get it," Bryce says as Lana walks away.

"No wonder she was a Vagrant," Cecil says under his breath.

Lana stops, straightening, and her grip on the staff tightens. I can see the tension in her shoulders. She turns and looks at the two humans sitting on the sand.

"What did you say?" she asks, emphasizing each word.

"What?" Cecil asks. "It's not like everyone doesn't know."

Emotions race across her face and moisture forms at the corners of her eyes. She grits her teeth, shakes her head, then turns her back on them. A tightness grips my chest, making it hard to get a deep breath. I know not what they speak of but I would hurt them for wounding my treasure.

"We're supposed to be hunting," she says, walking away.

I move closer. My stomach churns with a conflict of emotions. The human males look up at me, their eyes widening in fear.

"Hey, hey," Cecil says, holding his hands up and making a pushing motion towards me.

"We don't mean anything," Bryce says.

I shake my head and turn away. They are not worth it. Breaking into a jog I catch up with Lana. "Are you okay?"

"I'm fine," she says, shrugging her shoulders.

I nod, understanding that she may not be fine but she doesn't want to talk about it right now. Sometimes all you can do is be there for someone. I find it nice to have someone to be there for. I've spent so much time alone in the desert. I love the way her hair bounces off her shoulders as she walks. Her mind is as sharp as her beauty. We've been hunting together for a month now and she's learning fast. I'm impressed. There is a determination and strength to her I don't see in the other humans.

After a short silence, she mutters, "I'm amazed those two are still alive."

"How much longer do we have to be out here?" Bryce asks, trailing along behind us.

"Until we get food," Lana says.

At least these two aren't part of Gershom's faction. I haven't lived with the humans for long but that one I can't stand. He's dangerous. If Bryce and Cecil were part of his group, they wouldn't be speaking Zmaj. His 'human first' mentality would prevent it.

The suns overhead beat down, casting an angry red glow across the sand. Lana stops and opens her water bottle, taking a long drink then she pours some of the water over her head. "Damn, it's hot."

"It's not that bad," I reply.

"Of course it's not for you," she says. "Big, sexy, and covered in those beautiful scales. Your body is made for this. Mine is doing its best just to live."

Her body draws my attention in. What I wouldn't give to explore those luscious curves. Her anatomy is fascinating. So different from what I remember of Zmaj females.

"You think so?" I ask. She called me sexy. I know this human term for desirable.

"Think what?" Lana asks.

"Nothing," I say, feeling embarrassed.

She flashes a smile that makes me want her even more. I'm about to say something when the low cooing of the bivo sounds ahead. Lana and I exchange a quick glance.

"I'm so ready for this," she says, her enthusiasm shining.

"Remember, be careful," I reply.

"Why did we stop?" Cecil asks, coming up from behind.

Lana puts a finger on her full, sensuous lips, then walks the short distance to the top of the dune. At the base below is a herd of twelve bivo. The Alpha stands apart, watching his herd. The wind blows against us, keeping them from picking up our scent.

"Oh, shit," Bryce says, joining us at the ridge.

I take my lochaber off my back. Lana moves her staff to the ready.

"So, uh, how are we doing this?" Cecil asks.

Lana glances in my direction and I see the uncertainty in her eyes. She's been learning fast but practice with a weapon is a far cry from using it.

"You too," I say, pointing at Bryce and Cecil. "I want you both to go down the dune on that side. Do not approach the bivo. Just make sure they see you."

7

"And what happens then?" Bryce asks.

"You'll have the Alpha's attention," I grin.

"Um, isn't that going to be... bad?" Cecil asks.

"Depends," I say, shrugging. "How fast can you run?"

Lana snorts as the two boys' faces turn pale.

"Yeah we're not doing that," Bryce says.

"Don't you to get it?" Lana asks. "He's messing with you."

I smile, glad she picked up on it even if they didn't.

"I totally knew," Cecil says.

"You're a liar," Bryce replies.

"Enough," I say before they can degenerate into further arguing. "Bivo scare easy. We should be able to take down two or three of them before the herd runs."

"Yeah but how do we take them out?" Cecil asks.

"In all seriousness," I say, "I want the two of you to distract the Alpha."

"How do we do that?" Bryce asks.

"Pretty much what I said. The key is to not be threatening."

"Okay," Cecil says. "Don't be threatening, right, got it."

I detail out what I want them to do until I'm sure they've got it. Now it's just a matter of executing my plan. Lana kneels beside me while we wait for the boys to get into position.

I like having her here with me. She's comfortable in my space, like she belongs.

When I first arrived at Drakonov, I fought with Shidan over Amara. He and Amara are together now and that's good. I'm happy for them, I don't see it as a loss. I was in the grip of bijass then, that primal instinct which dwells within every Zmaj male. Amara was never the right one for me. I only fought for her so the other male couldn't have her. Later, when I first saw Lana, I knew. She's the one. Now I have to wait for her to figure it out.

Cecil and Bryce walked out into the view of the bivo Alpha. While his herd continues routing in the red sand for roots and food, the Alpha turns his attention. Lana's breathing speeds up. She tightens her grip on her staff, preparing.

The two boys push and shove each other then stumble out into the open. Cecil curses Bryce and the Alpha reacts to the commotion. Lana and I watch, waiting for the right moment. Cecil and Bryce look at each other, say something I can't hear, then shrug. They're staring at the bivo herd as they move sideways further out into the open.

Rising, I move forward with my lochaber at the ready. Lana moves alongside me. We creep forward, keeping an eye on the Alpha. The danger with bivo is twofold. A stampede is the first concern. Even the smallest bivo here is two to three times my weight, a herd of them running full speed would trample the four of us.

The main concern, however, is the Alpha. Bivo are herd animals, not smart or aware of their surroundings. They survive by breeding fast and often, birthing more than the predators that feed on them can eat. Only the Alpha of a herd is a fighter.

He stands out with his long, curled horns which end in sharp points that protrude from either side of his head. The horns are deadly and the animal will be skilled in their use. My intention is to get close enough to the herd to kill two, maybe three, before the Alpha is aware, then cause a stampede.

Once the herd is running he'll go along with them, leaving us with our prize of meat. I've done this hundreds of times before but always for a single bivo. Attempting more will be a challenge. We have to kill them fast before they raise an alarm.

Hot breath of a beast blasts across me as we get close

enough to do our job. It looks at us with large, empty black eyes before putting its head back down to root in the sand.

"Awww," Lana says.

I move beside it, place the blade of my lochaber along its throat, then pull across in a single motion. Hot blood sprays across my hands, spilling onto the sand.

"Ugh!" Lana cries out and all the bivo stop, raising their large heads to look.

A loud snort, a stomp that breaks through the low sounds of the moving herd, and I know we're in trouble. Lana, eyes wide and face covered in blood spray, shakes her head side to side.

"SHIT!" Cecil screams. "RUN!"

I whirl my lochaber over my head and jump in front of Lana. The Alpha is charging through the herd, pushing them aside as he bears down on us.

"Run Lana," I hiss. "Run now!"

She doesn't move, damn it. What is wrong with her?

The Alpha is too close. There's no time. I can't dodge to one side and strike at it, that would leave Lana exposed. Whirling around, I knock her feet out from under her with my tail and catch her in my arms as I turn. Keeping the motion going I drop to the ground encircling her with my body to protect her as I roll us out of the path of the charging Alpha.

The thunder of its broad hooves causes the sand to dance as it passes. I keep rolling until the momentum won't carry us any further up the dune. Coming to a stop with her underneath me, I look for the Alpha.

It's staring up the dune, pawing at the ground, not ready to give up yet. A glint of steel shines from behind it, my lochaber where I had to let it go to save Lana.

A dozen options race through my mind and I discard each. I rise to a crouch and keep Lana behind me. The Alpha and I stare into each other's eyes. There is dim intelligence to the beast. I spread my wings, lean forward, and hiss. The Alpha stomps the ground, snorts, then shakes his head side to side. I slap the sand in front of me, flap my wings, and hiss louder.

The Alpha and I stare at each other. A contest of wills. I flap my wings and rise to my full height. Throwing my arms wide, I roar and stomp the ground with my foot. The Alpha takes a step back so I take one forward. I continue to flap my wings, my tail shifting side to side, as I stalk forward. I lean into my stride, making myself as threatening as possible. I hiss then follow it with a roar. The Alpha continues to retreat. The herd around him lows, uncertain, the Alpha isn't supposed to retreat. He shakes his head side to side, lowering his horns down until they're scraping the sand. I stop advancing, waiting. The Alpha turns and runs. The herd falls in behind, leaving us alone.

"I'm sorry," Lana says, her soft touch on my shoulder.

"It's fine," I say. "At least we got one."

"One won't feed us for long," she says, shaking her head.

"Let tomorrow's problem be tomorrow's problem."

"Damn," Bryce says as the two boys approach. "That was the most amazing thing I've ever seen."

"You're like, super bad ass," Cecil adds.

"It was impressive," Lana agrees.

Warm heat surges through my cock at her words. My cheeks burn. I shrug and smile, trying to down play it. "It was nothing."

"It was a hell of a lot more than nothing," Lana says. "I guess you're my hero now."

My hearts skip a beat. She touches my chest and my scales flush hot. Her warm brown eyes draw me closer. I lean in, unsure of what I'm doing. Her full lips part and the wild desire to see what the human mouth mating is like consumes me. We're close, so close, I can claim what I want.

She laughs and shakes her head, breaking the moment. My treasure steps away as the world spins around. Strange how I feel crushed. I doubt it would feel worse if the bivo had run me over.

"So how do we get this thing home?" Lana asks.

Inhaling deeply, I roll my shoulders then set about preparing the kill for travel.

2

LANA

*W*e're back from the hunt and I'm tired but I don't want to be alone so I'm hanging out with the paired up couples and some other girls. I like getting to see people actually happy and the new little baby is the most adorbs thing ever.

"There is no way in hell I'm doing that," Amara states, breaking into my thoughts.

"You won't have a choice," Calista replies.

"How can you not want this?" Jolie says from her position, propped up in the makeshift bed of furs Sverre built. This little group has commandeered the lower floor of the 'command' building that's just off the city center fountain. "It's wonderful."

"What is wonderful, my love?" Sverre asks as he walks up and hands her a waterskin.

"You are," she says, rising and puckering her lips.

Sverre leans in and takes her kiss. She seems so happy, even if she is as big as a house. Jolie is in the last stages of her pregnancy and has had to be on bed rest for the last two weeks.

"Because I like doing things for myself?" Amara says. "What is wrong with that? I don't need nobody to wait on me hand and foot. Besides, I have work to do."

"Well I like it," Jolie says. "It makes me feel like a princess."

"You are my treasure," Sverre says.

"All right you two," Mei says. "Get a room already."

Everyone laughs.

"Why is being stuck in bed and treated like an invalid necessary?" Amara asks.

Our resident nerds, Calista and Jolie, exchange a glance. Calista clears her throat, takes a drink of water, then schools her face into her best lecture giving pose. "We're built for nine months of pregnancy, more or less," Calista says. "But the Zmaj have much bigger bodies than humans."

"Well that much is obvious," Amara says.

I find myself jealous of Amara. She's so blunt and brash. It's not so much that I want to be like that but her attitude, the certainty of herself and that she belongs. I've never had that. Somehow I got lucky enough to be friends with this group. They accept me as I am, without question, even with my background on the ship.

"Well basic biology tells us that the bigger the body the longer the gestation," Calista continues. "You're carrying a hybrid, Zmaj and human, so the pregnancy will take longer. I was pregnant for thirteen months and Jolie is already past that. After the nine or ten that our bodies are used to, it starts to really strain and we have to stay rested and off our feet. I learned that the hard way."

"Well that make sense," Mei says.

"I don't care if it makes sense," Amara grouses. "I have a lot to do and can't lie around for months."

"Or more, but I don't see where you have a choice," Calista says.

"This sucks," Amara says.

"Maybe it won't be so bad," Shidan, Amara's mate, adds while rubbing her back.

I can tell by the huge smile on his face that he's excited by the idea. I don't know what he sees in Amara. She's strong, independent, and also abrasive as hell. He loves her though, that much is obvious.

"Wouldn't it be nice if we had music?" Inga asks.

"Yes it would wouldn't it?" Jolie adds.

The easy buzz of conversation fills the room. Everyone is having a good time. I find a place to relax and sit and enjoy the atmosphere. The others may take it for granted, having friends, people who care about you, but I don't. I value it and am grateful to be a part of this group.

"Did you see that?" Mei asks.

"What?" Jolie asks, shifting her position on the bed to follow Mei's gaze.

"Illadon, he rolled over!" Mei says.

Conversation stops as everyone looks. Illadon is in the middle of the floor staring back at everyone with wide eyes from his position on his tiny, scaled belly. He smiles then flutters his wings. My heart melts as the sound of oohs and ahhs fill the room. Illadon is cute, too cute for words.

Calista walks over to her baby and kneels. Ladon looks on, beaming with pride, his large arms crossed over his chest. Everyone waits for a repeat performance. The only sound is the swish of Illadon's tiny tail on the carpet. He flutters his wings again then holds his hands up towards his mother.

"Are you going to roll over?" Calista asks the child.

Illadon giggles.

"Here, let me help you," his mother says.

She takes Illadon and gently rolls him back to his back. His chunky legs wobble back and forth as he struggles to get back on his stomach. A look of intense concentration comes over his face. The way his little brow furrows causes his scales to catch the light, forming a rainbow of color. He looks up at his mother.

"Come on baby," Calista encourages him.

I'm holding my breath without realizing it. Everyone is waiting, it's a special moment, and we're about to share it together. Illadon grunts, then hisses, then he's on his side. Excitement wells up inside me until I'm sure I will burst. Inside I'm cheering him on.

"Come on son," Ladon says, his voice filled with pride.

Illadon's wings push against the floor. His tiny tongue darts out between his lips then his arm is underneath him and smoothly rolls back to his belly. He pushes himself up with his hands and beams.

The room explodes with applause. Illadon looks startled, unsure of what all the commotion is about. He frowns and for a moment he's scared then I see his eyes lock with his dad and he grins. It's obvious he loves being the center of attention.

"Good job baby," Calista says.

Illadon returns to playing with the makeshift toys everyone has found for him. Calista rises and turns back to Amara. "Anyway, Amara, bed rest is the only answer."

"Yet another reason this place sucks," Amara says.

The Zmaj males glance at each other.

"But you have me," Shidan says, trying to lighten the mood.

"That I do," Amara agrees, sighing. "It doesn't mean I don't wish the rest of the planet didn't suck so hard."

"Welcome to Vulcan," Calista says, shrugging.

"It's Gallifrey!" Jolie shouts from her bed.

"You're both wrong, it's hell," Amara says. "The only good thing is, I've been a really bad girl."

Amara grins at Shidan and pulls him into a passionate kiss. Only then do I notice Astarot stands apart from the group. I doubt the others even see him. Maybe it's just one outcast recognizing another. He watches, listens, but doesn't take part. There's a small ache in my chest when I look at him.

"Anyone know where Rosalind is?" Mei asks.

"I told the Lady General we were getting together," Inga replies. "She said she might stop by."

I'm drawn to Astarot. An emptiness surrounds him. He smiles, nods, the other men talk, but he remains separate.

Inga sits down next to me. "Are you okay?" she asks.

Startled I glance over. "What do you mean?"

Inga shrugs. "Nothing, I guess. I mean…"

The way she trails pulls my attention. "What Inga?" I ask, keeping my voice soft.

The buzz of conversation continues. This is life, life as we know it now. People are adjusting to our new circumstances. No more bars, no more restaurants for dinner, but these small gatherings are becoming commonplace among the survivors.

"It's just, I don't want to, oh, I don't know."

"Okay, well that's a dodge. Don't know what? What is it you want to say?"

"Well on the ship you were… you know."

"A vagrant?" I ask.

Inga blushes bright red telling me all I need to know. Anger flashes, white hot, but it goes as fast as it comes. That's the old me. The outcast, the one who didn't belong. I stare, waiting for her to say what she wants to say. Confirm or deny.

"Yes," she says, somehow she turns an even deeper shade of red.

"I was," I agree. "What of it?"

"I just… I meant nothing by it. I only wanted to see how you are."

I smile and the flush on her face lightens. She exhales an obvious sigh of relief that I'm not raging angry.

"Thank you," I say. "That's kind."

"It's, I mean, sure," she says, stumbling over her words.

"I'm doing fine."

"What was it like?" she asks. "I can't imagine how hard it must have been for you."

Shaking my head, I smile, but inside the pain is still there. The deep wound of knowing the world you live in doesn't want you. I can't deny it left a mark on me.

"I had my mom," I say.

"You did? I thought all vagrants were..."

I nod. "They are but my real mom died birthing me. The doctor who delivered me, she adopted me and raised me as her own."

"Oh, that's very nice," Inga says.

I shrug. "She was a good woman."

"I'm glad you had someone."

Anyone else would offend me with that statement. I've heard it before and it's always made me angry, but Inga is so genuine, so real, her care and concern surrounds me.

"Thank you."

Inga smiles then holds her arms out so I hug her.

"I'm glad you're here with us," Inga says as we part, she smiles and it warms my heart.

"Me too," I say.

Out of the corner of my eye I see Astarot watching from across the room. He's big and strong, like all the Zmaj, but the coloring of his scales is gorgeous. His eyes are brilliant, almost a purple color, and they flash with deep intelligence. Slippery wetness slides between my thighs. I'm not ready for a long term relationship but it doesn't mean I don't have needs.

"If you need anything," Inga says. "Tell me, okay?"

"Sure," I smile. "I appreciate it."

I do, too. On the ship no one was nice. I was outcast, unwanted, no purpose and no use. I was a useless drain on resources. There was little surplus and no room for error. Everyone else on the ship had a job, a purpose in the grand scheme of things. Vagrants, like me, did not. My days were spent avoiding people's dark glares and trying to survive. There were times I wished I'd never been born. There was strict population control and most unplanned pregnancies never made it.

My mom, my birth mom, hid her pregnancy though, until it was too late. We were too 'civilized' to end a pregnancy once it had reached the second trimester. No, much more humane to let that child grow up outcast and unwanted. If not for my adopted mom, I wouldn't have survived anyway. The majority of vagrants don't make it past their teens. Forced to live on the edges of society, they either starved to death or died in some other way.

The world on the ship was against a vagrant. Ingrained into the culture of ship life. Vagrants are a drain, have no purpose, and they don't belong. Get rid of the vagrants, send them back to, well, wherever as long as 'normal' people didn't have to worry about it.

"Hey," Inga says.

"Yeah?"

"You were drifting away, you sure you're okay?" she asks, concerned.

"Yeah," I say, shaking myself free of the memories and the pain. "Yeah, I'm fine."

"You going to talk to him?"

"Who?"

"Astarot," she smiles.

"What are you talking about?"

"Don't play coy," she says. "You two have been making eyes at each other all night."

"He has?" I ask, my heart skipping a beat.

"He has!" she laughs.

"Oh, well then," I grin.

"Have fun," Inga says, rising and going over to check on Jolie.

I stand up and make my way across the common area towards Astarot.

"So, come here often?" I ask.

"Only when I'm invited," Astarot says.

I shake my head and chuckle. Sometimes the simple things get lost in translation from Common to Zmaj.

"Yeah," I say, meeting his eyes.

I love his eyes. They're gorgeous, deep pools of lavender, I could lose myself in them. A slow smile forms on his face and I touch him without thinking about it. His face is cool and I'm surprised by how smooth it is. I'm not sure what I expected. I guess I thought his scales would be rough. I can feel their edges as I run my fingers along but they're not rough at all.

Complex emotions dance in his beautiful eyes. His jaw tightens as his wings flutter and his thick, scaled tail thumps into the wall. I pull my hand back, realizing how bold and forward I'm being. I'm not shy with men but even I have my limits. I don't know what came over me. He blinks several times and I wonder if he's clearing his thoughts before he berates me. He swallows hard then shakes his head.

"Uhm," he says, doing nothing to break the awkwardness.

"Sorry," I say, quick, trying to move past my embarrassment.

"No!" he says, too loud.

Conversation stops. My back burns hot, I know they're all

staring at us. My cheeks flush warm as I purse my lips and look down at the ground. I hate being the center of attention.

"You okay?" Calista asks, walking up and looking between the two of us.

I'm not sure who she's addressing, Astarot or me, but I answer, wanting to get past this.

"Yeah, it's fine," I say, looking up at Astarot and begging with my eyes.

"Sorry," he says. Is he blushing? The edges of his scales are turning a shade of red, is that how a Zmaj flushes? "I was only responding to a question, I did not mean to be so loud."

Conversations resume behind us as the moment passes. Calista looks between the two of us with her sharp, perceptive eyes. She bites her lower lip. A half smile forms then she nods, placing a hand on each of our arms.

"If either of you need… anything," she pauses for effect before continuing. "I'm here for you."

Astarot looks confused by the offer but I see it for what it is. She's playing matchmaker. I smile, shake my head, then put my hand on her shoulder.

"Thank you, but we're fine," I say, nice but firm, hoping to end any bright ideas.

"Of course you are," she says, the smile on her face saying so much more than her words.

Calista walks away but not without a sidelong glance over her shoulder. She walks straight over to Jolie, all propped up in her furs and scavenged blankets, and leans in close to whisper. Great, now they're both playing matchmaker.

"I do not understand," Astarot says.

"Don't worry about it," I sigh. "It's a girl thing."

"A 'girl thing'?" he asks, making it obvious I'm just confusing him even more.

"Yeah," I smile, giving him my full attention.

I don't miss the way his gaze drops to my cleavage. Even

if I've got nothing else in this life, I'm well blessed by the tits gods and I make damn good use of them. Show just the right amount of skin and you can get most any man to do anything you want. Some women, too. I don't hold it against them, its basic biology, and I don't feel bad for anything I've done. Biology also demands I eat and survive.

Once I was old enough to be on my own, I didn't want to depend on my adopted mother for my basic needs. On the ship everyone had an allotment of food and supplies. Adopting a vagrant didn't get you a bigger share. As my need for food and supplies increased, so too did the strain on her resources, not that she'd ever say a word about it.

A pang of loss hits me out of nowhere. I try not to think about Bailey too much, or what happened to her. I suppose the best I can hope for is that she died quickly. It's the one thing none of us talks about, those we lost when the pirates attacked our generation ship. Only one section of it crashed here, the part we were in. What became of the rest of the massive ship no one knows. We assume they were all killed. Thinking about the pirates, I hope they were. The thought of my mom being in the hands of those monsters is more than I can stand.

"Okay," he says, his eyes locked on mine.

"Astarot," Sverre calls from behind us.

"Yes?" he asks, but his eyes never leave mine.

"What did you do before?"

"I worked on the docks," Astarot replies.

"Dock worker, huh?" I grin. "So you're used to handling large packages?"

"Very much so," he says.

I'm not sure if he understood my innuendo or not. Zmaj are literal, it's the nature of their language and it would seem their culture too. Or maybe he got it? The way he's looking into my eyes, the grin on his face, I think he might have.

"Where at?" Sverre asks.

Astarot answers but I'm not listening anymore. All my attention is on studying his face. The strong jaw, his full lips, the way they move when he talks. The way his eyes never leave mine, even as he's talking with Sverre. I decide, this moment, that tonight Astarot is going to get lucky.

"How about a walk?" he asks.

It takes a moment for me to realize he's talking to me, not them. Then I have to take another moment to process the sounds into words. Now things are becoming awkward. I clear my throat then look away.

"That'd be nice," I say.

We say our good nights to our friends and leave the apartment. Their eyes are on us as we do but to hell with them. It's better than the negative attention I'm used to and I know they only want the best for us.

3

ASTAROT

*T*he thunder in my ear from my racing hearts makes conversation difficult as we walk out of the building, side by side. As we step from the shadows into the open air, the heat wraps us like a warm embrace.

"Ugh," Lana gasps.

"Are you okay?"

"Yeah, the heat gets me every time," she says.

"You're taking the epis?"

"Yeah, it's not awful, not like it used to be. It still takes my breath away though," she smiles.

"I'm glad it's getting better," I say.

The suns are setting and their last rays make the protective dome over the city sparkle, creating thin rainbows of color as the light breaks down into its parts.

"I love sunset," she says. "It's so beautiful."

"Have you gone to a roof and watched?" I ask.

"No, I haven't ever had the chance," she says.

"Let's go!"

She reaches out her hand. It's tiny and soft as it lies engulfed in my own. I meet her eyes, gorgeous, rich eyes that are so full of life. We smile and the primal urge to claim her leaps up as does my cock. I lean closer, wanting to have the mating of mouths I've seen the others do. The lids of Lana's eyes drift down until they are half-closed, my desire rages as we come closer together.

Our lips meet. A jolt races through my body from my lips out through my limbs. As quick as they meet we part. She leans back as I straighten. She looks away as do I, did I offend her? Uncertainty pounds in my head.

"Which way?" she asks, no hint of admonishment or upset.

Her hand is still in mine so she must not mind, right? Did she like it? Before more uncertainty can beset me I lead the way to a building on the edge of the city proper. It's not far, a few blocks, that we traverse with good speed. The buildings in this section of the city are still empty, rotting. Broken shards of old windows lines the street, the exteriors are falling apart, showing signs of age, neglect, and where roaming animals once marked their territory.

I lead us into the dim interior of an ancient structure. The suns are setting fast so we have to hurry to catch the sight I want to share. We wind our way through debris, rotting furniture and parts of the ceiling that have collapsed.

"Damn, this is dark," Lana says as we make our way further in.

The lighting isn't a problem for me but she squints then blink several times.

"I didn't think to bring a light," I say.

I knew humans didn't see well in the dark but I forgot. She moves closer, an unexpected benefit that makes me smile. Her warmth against my scales is more pleasurable than I would have imagined. I want her to be this close always. Thoughts of wrapping her in my arms, pulling her close, and holding her forever cloud my mind. Intoxicated with my own thoughts the climb passes quickly. At the top of the building is a rusted door highlighted by streams of light shining through rotted holes. I push but it doesn't open. Leaning my weight in, the door screeches open with the sound of metal dragging against metal.

"Thought you'd been here before?" she asks.

"I have, sand still gets through the dome," I explain.

"Ah," she says.

I move through the door ahead of her then hear her gasp, turning just in time to see her mouth fall open then she turns a circle. Placing her hands over her mouth she shakes herself then walks towards the edge of the roof.

The view is stunning, which is why I brought her here. The dual red suns are setting on the horizon, peeking over the mountain range in the far distance. Their final, blazing rays cause the sand to sparkle like a perfect gem. Brilliant reds, whites, and arcing lines of blue dance across the rolling dunes towards the city. The dome over the city that keeps out predators filters the light and turns it into a dreamy haze.

"You like it?" I ask.

"Like it? It's... stunning."

My smile is so wide my jaw hurts but I don't care. My scales tingle with excitement because my treasure is pleased. She turns towards me, placing her hands on my chest, looking up into my eyes. The warmth of her hands spreads across my scales. She rises and I'm pulled into her like a gravity well until our lips meet. Everything focuses into that singular point of contact where we are becoming one. Her arms move over my shoulders, wrapping around my neck. I put my arms around her waist, pulling her tighter against me. Her body melds to mine as our mating of mouths continues.

She pulls back gasping in air then she kisses across my jaw. Her hot tongue drags along the line of my neck. My hands drop to her full ass, running over her curves. My first cock stiffens to the point I might explode before we do anything.

The soft mounds of her large breasts press hard against my chest, moving as she does, enticing. Her hips move against mine and I grind into her. Desire rules the day, I want to make her mine. I lift her up, bringing her closer, her legs wrap around my waist. My cock presses against the cloth of my pants, straining for her.

She moans as her hips grind against my dick. I pull her head back from where she is kissing my neck. Our lips come together with bruising force. My grip in her hair holds us together. Her tongue licks my lips then presses past them into my mouth. My tongue rises to meet hers in a dance. Her pussy is so close, grinding against my cock. I need her. Pressure builds in my core until I'm sure I can't wait any longer.

Her hand drives between us until it finds my cock. She works her way into my pants and takes my dick in a firm grip. She strokes up and down. I close my eyes concentrating to avoid the impending explosion. She unwraps her legs so I lower her back to her feet. Pulling her hands out of my pants she runs her hands across my chest. She lowers herself before me, dragging her hands along my body as she does.

In moments my pants are dropping to the ground and my cock springs free. She takes it in a hand but her small, human hand isn't big enough to wrap around it. Her light touch strokes the soft underside. Looking up, she smiles, then runs her tongue along my shaft.

"Oh!" I cry out in surprise and pleasure.

New sensations race through my body unlike anything I've felt before. My first load explodes, pumping out onto her and the ground between us as she strokes and runs her tongue along my shaft. She doesn't stop until I'm spent.

"Good?" she asks, rising until her lips are next to mine.

"Beyond," I say.

I work the buttons of her shirt then pull it over her shoulders. When it drops off, I move my head back so I can see her enticing mounds. A Zmaj woman's breasts had hard plates that protected them which opened only for feeding babies. Lana's are out all the time, which is fascinating, and Lana's look larger than the other women's too. I've fantasized about what they might look like under her clothing.

Some kind of white cloth with straps that run over her shoulders covers them still. I slide the straps down but the cloth doesn't drop. She presses her mouth to mine, pulling my attention. Our tongues meet and dance but I continue to explore her beauty with my hands. My second cock is rising, straining between us now, but I ignore it, focusing what attention I can on her breasts.

Hooking my fingers under the cloth that is still protecting them I pull it back. It stretches but doesn't come loose so I pull it down and at last her breasts are exposed. I lower my head. The centers are light brown, circular, with bumps. On instinct I tease them with my tongue then take one in my mouth. A hard point forms so I nibble on that. Lana moans, her hands grabbing my head and holding me tight against her.

Moving over to the other I go back and forth and she groans louder. Keeping most of my attention on her breasts with my hands, I work at her pants until they drop free. One handed I rub between her thighs. Another piece of cloth covers her mound, it feels thin, so I grab the sides and slide it off.

Touching the soft fur that grows on her mound I can feel wetness coming from her. She is ready for mating and I want to, but I hold off. I press one finger into the opening past her soft lips and push it into her wetness. I continue licking and teasing her breasts while exploring her delicate folds with my finger.

"Astarot," she pants, thrusting her hips forward and driving my finger deeper.

She's tight around my finger, gripping it hard, I wonder if I can fit into her without harming her. I know the other Zmaj males have done so, but I don't want to hurt Lana. I will let her lead to be sure I do not harm her.

Her hips thrust back then forward driving my finger in and out so I comply. Moving it faster, she pants louder and louder. I lick her breasts in time with the thrusting of my fingers. My lips lock onto the hard point and pull then switch to the other and repeat.

Her groans become a constant chant of wordless sounds of pleasure. As her body adjusts to my finger inside her, it becomes wetter. I slide a second finger in, expanding her, preparing her for my cock. It slides in easy but again feels tight. She groans as she moves her hips back and forth.

She pulls on the back of my head. I look up and she leans in, pressing her lips to mine and groans into my mouth. As her body adjusts and the wetness increases, I add a third finger. She gasps in surprise but the panting groans continue.

Deciding she is ready I hook my hands under her ass and lift her up. My second cock is ready, throbbing with desire. Moving slow while continuing to kiss I lower her down until I feel the first hints of her wetness touching my cock. She throws her head back and sighs as I continue lowering her.

The head of my cock pushes into her until the first ridge on top of my cock meets resistance. The pressure of her sliding down increases and then with surprising suddenness, the first ridge is enveloped by her tightness. She yelps and I stop, worried.

When she opens her eyes and meets mine, she bites her

lower lip then nods. I resume lowering her onto my dick. Nothing has ever felt better. Her body grips me, welcoming me, it's a sensation like coming home after a long, hard day. I groan as I slide deeper into her until at last my cock is buried. The hard ridge at the base on my pelvis probes into her soft folds. She shifts her hips then gasps, her eyes widen, and she smiles.

"Oh god!" she exclaims, rotating her hips in a circle.

Her grip on my shoulders tightens. Smashing her lips into mine, our teeth click together, then her tongue is driving into my mouth as she pulls herself up then drops back down on my cock.

She sets a fast, hard rhythm, one I never would have tried. Rising and falling on my dick. My core tightens until it's a hard ball. I'm struggling to maintain my control, she feels so good.

"Astarot," she grunts my name with each downward thrust.

As she lowers herself taking me in, she throws her head back and lets out a wordless cry of pleasure. I answer her cry with my own as we become one. Our bodies joining in the physical manifestation as our souls entwine with each other.

She puts her head on my shoulder, panting. I can feel her pounding heart against my chest. As her heart rate slows and she regains her breath she moves, raising her head and pulling herself up. I assist her, taking her off my cock, and lowering her to the ground.

"That was fun," she smiles.

"Yes," I agree, as we both gather our clothing and dress.

She pulls her shirt on then stops to stare out at the encroaching shadows. The suns have dipped below the horizon, only their reflected light pushes back the darkness.

"It's beautiful," she exhales.

"I think so," I say, stepping over to her and putting an arm around her waist.

"Okay, well I'll see you tomorrow," she says as she turns and walks towards the door.

"Uh, what?" I ask.

The sudden shift in attitude and the words make no sense. We joined, there is much to discuss, what is she doing?

"I'll see you tomorrow?" she asks, confusion obvious on her face.

"But, we joined," I say.

"Yes, and it was fun," she replies.

"I do not understand."

She looks confused too. She shakes her head then tilts it to one side. "I have to butcher tomorrow. Aren't you going to be there?" she asks.

Butcher? The meat? She's talking about the meat, but what about us?

"But... what about... we joined?" I ask, feeling lost.

"Yes," she says shaking her head. "It's a hook-up. A one night stand, right?"

"A... one night stand?" I've never heard of such a thing. I know the words but putting them together makes no sense.

"Yeah, you know, we had fun, now we go on with our lives?"

"Oh," I say.

My hearts quit beating. A hard pressure squeezes my chest, it's impossible to breathe.

"You okay?" she asks, showing signs of concern.

Swallowing hard, I nod. "Yes," I say, my voice on the edge of cracking.

"Okay, good," she says, turning and walking through the door.

Watching her leave a wave of nausea passes over me. I bend over and rest my hands on my knees until it passes.

One night stand? I think to myself.

Zmaj don't do... whatever that is. When we join, we're

31

joined, that's it. It's the culmination. Dealing with humans is so... strange. I want her, I need her. I can't imagine life without her. She is my treasure. So what do I do?

I do what I have to do. If this is what I can have of her, then I will take it. The only other option I see is to not have her at all but that is not an option. She needs time, that must be the answer. I will wait.

She will see, she's my treasure and we'll be together. It's only a matter of time.

Resolved, I walk over to the edge of the building and stare out across the dim lit dunes. Clouds are rolling in, making the shadows deeper than normal. I left my home to find something. Not knowing what, but I knew I'd know it when I saw it and I did, the moment I found Lana.

No matter what comes against us, I'll be there for her. No matter how long I have to wait for her, I will. Her and her kind have brought hope back to this desolate wasteland. Before the humans came, I waited not only for my own extinction but that of my race as well.

Sverre and Calista have a child now. That is more hope than I would have ever thought possible. Jolie will birth soon. In time, Lana will see, and we will have our own hatchling. It is our duty to make the world a better place for them. They should not have to live in a wasteland like this. Once, the Zmaj civilization was strong and we can make it such again.

Something flashes on the horizon. I close my outer lids to filter the light but it doesn't repeat. Something is out there, I'm certain of it. I will arrange a patrol for tomorrow and look in that direction. I can't allow the Zzlo slavers to take us by surprise.

Resolved, I make my way back to my apartment where I lie down, alone. *It won't be long,* I think as I drift off to sleep.

4

LANA

Stupid! Stupid! Stupid! I think, hacking at the meat in front of me.

I shouldn't have slept with him. The look in his eyes when I left, damn it. I like him, a lot, but I'm not looking to settle down or commit to anyone right now. Why did I let that happen? Biology of course. I had an itch, he's a great guy, and then nature takes its course.

"Hey, take it easy," Bert says.

I look down at the meat I've been working on and see what a mess I've made of it.

"Sorry," I say.

"It's fine, let's not waste it though okay?"

Everyone is looking at me. Of course they are, I'm the vagrant. I'm the one that doesn't belong. I'm not supposed to be here. But that was on the ship. Here, on Tajss, I have an opportunity and I will take full advantage of it.

"No problem," I say, smiling at Bert.

I touch his hand and bat my eyes and I'm rewarded with a smile. One of the other women butchering mutters something under her breath I don't catch. It doesn't matter.

Sooner or later they'll figure it out, they need me. I'll make sure of it.

Bert moves on, checking the work of the other people who are helping. We have no way of storing meat for an extended period. The Zmaj use oiled leathers and a drying technique to make it last longer but it does nothing for the flavor. I don't mind, although the others complain. It's what they do, complain. I think I'm the only one who doesn't hate being here.

"This place sucks," a woman named Sarah says from nearby like she's reading my mind.

I don't know her well, just a passing acquaintance. I don't miss the ship. There I had no purpose, unwanted, and did what I had to do to survive. There are so few of us survivors here on Tajss that none of that matters anymore. Well, it won't once they realize it. People cling to the old ways as much as they can.

"Have any of you heard about what Gershom's saying?" Sarah asks.

"What now?" I ask, rolling my eyes.

"You know she'd act that way," a woman I don't know mutters and my cheeks burn at her jab.

"He's saying we should have a vote," Sarah answers.

"A vote about what?" Bert asks, walking by.

"President, what else?" Sarah asks.

"About damn time," another man, Jacob, mutters.

"Who cares?" Cecil chimes in.

"What do you mean who cares?" Sarah asks. "We're a democracy, its core to our values, if we lose that then what do we have?"

"I'll vote for anyone who will shorten the work day," Bryce says and Cecil laughs along with him.

Some of the others snort at his joking.

"Shorten the work day," Bert shakes his head. "You'd have to actually do some work first Bryce."

"Hey!" Bryce says, holding up a jagged piece of meat and waving it in the air, flinging gore around. "What do you think this is?"

"A badly cut piece of meat that might be salvageable," Bert barks. "Did you not watch anything I showed you!"

"What are you talking about? This is perfect, like prime rib or something," Bryce replies.

"Prime rib my ass," Bert growls, stalking over to Bryce.

"I like Rosalind," Mei says, returning attention to the original topic while Bert takes Bryce's knife away and shows him again how to slice the meat. Mei is impeccable, she looks perfect and clean and composed and I stare down at the mess I've made as the conversation continues.

"What a surprise," the same woman who was jabbing at me says.

"What is that supposed to mean Enid?" Mei asks.

Enid, now I know her name. I think her and Jacob are brother and sister. She doesn't look up from the meat she's wrapping in oiled leathers, only shakes her head and ignores Mei's question.

"Who elected her?" Sarah asks, filling the void.

"What does that matter?" Mei asks. "She's the one who's kept us alive."

"This isn't living, this sucks," Cecil says.

I like Rosalind too. She's a good leader, she considers the good in everyone. Besides, Gershom is a dick. I can't stand his *Human First* movement. He's a petty asshole who couldn't get laid in a whorehouse with a thousand credits in his account.

"She's the one encouraging the cross-breeding," Jacob says.

Great, he's one of them. Gershom's rhetoric is 'Human

First'. They're anti-Zmaj and especially anti-human women falling in love with one. They don't seem to notice or care that without them we'd all be dead. Nope, doesn't matter in their small-minded, hate-filled hearts. They want to make sure that all the women are for them, which is what I think is really their problem.

"You can't control love," Mei says.

"Love?" Jacob snorts, his face turns bright red then edges towards purple. "That's not love! It's perverse! Unnatural! Disgusting cross-breeding that's led to one abomination already. It will be the death of our entire race!"

My grip tightens on the knife in my hand as my stomach churns with acid and my arms shake.

"That's enough!" Bert says, turning his back on Bryce and facing the room.

"All I'm saying is an election seems like a good idea," Sarah shrugs.

"If your Rosalind is so damn wonderful, why would she fear an election?" Enid asks, not looking up from her work.

"Who said she's scared of it?" Mei asks.

Are Mei and I the only Rosalind supporters in the room? I look at each of the others. There are ten people here. Mei and I are in Rosalind's camp I know. Jacob, Enid, and it seems Sarah are for Gershom. Bryce and Cecil, I doubt they're paying attention or care. Bert, I'm not sure. He plays his cards close to his chest. The other two, I think they're a couple, work in silence. I can't read them.

This could be bad. Does Rosalind know what Gershom is pushing for? I need to see her as soon as we're done here. She needs to know what's happening. One thing I'm certain of about Gershom, it's all about the power. He doesn't care about his 'causes', he looks for rallying points he can get people behind. I know men and the way he looks at me and every other woman tells it all. He sees women as meat,

36

objects for his use or pleasure. He may wear a mask that fools some but I see through it.

"Seems like you did," Enid says.

Enid looks haggard. It's obvious she isn't taking epis. Epis, the lifeblood of Tajss. A strange, glowing plant, hard to harvest but the only way humans can adjust to life on Tajss. Downside is, if you take it, you're stuck here. It's addictive. As in, it will kill you if you stop taking it. Most of Gershom's followers refuse to take it because it's 'alien'. It is, but not taking it is living a pipe dream. No one will rescue us. This is our home and the sooner they come to terms with that the better off we'll all be.

"I didn't say that," Mei breathes. "It's not fear or anything else. I'm just being practical. We're barely surviving as it is, why create a rift with an election?"

"Because we're a free people who should be able to have a say in our futures?" Enid retorts.

She looks tired. Her skin is lax with a gray tint to it. She squints her eyes as if we're out in the bright suns not indoors in a dim lit room. She's in extreme dehydration. Tajss is hot, too hot for humans to survive without epis. Epis changes you, on a molecular level or something. Calista and Jolie have talked about it but I couldn't follow their science talk. Sounded like a weird episode of Star Trek or something. I never could get into those shows.

All I know is epis makes me feel better. I don't have the headaches or the nausea or any of the other effects of dehydration. I can go out hunting with Astarot and as long as I take epis every two or three days the heat isn't killer. I heard them theorizing that it extends life too, which is why the Zmaj are so old.

"But you do!" Mei answers Enid.

"Do we?" Enid says, shaking her head. "I don't recall the

last time my opinion was asked about anything, not since the ship crashed."

"But," Mei says, then trails off.

All eyes in the room are on her as if they're waiting for some brilliant response. Problem is, there isn't one. I know it and so does Mei. Rosalind has been the de facto leader since the crash. On the ship she was the Lady General. Since we crashed, she has led by default. No one questioned it until now.

"That's what I thought," Enid says. "Maybe it's foreign to you, you're on the Secret Council or whatever you all call yourselves. I haven't sat down at any table or had any say in my life."

"It's not like that," Mei says, but her argument carries no force.

"Those of us out here," Enid motions around the room at the others, "we get told to work. Given jobs we might or might not choose for ourselves. Told it's for the 'greater good'. The almighty Rosalind, in her expansive wisdom, has ordered it so."

"But you don't have to-"

"Don't have to what? What would happen if one of us said no?" Enid cuts her off.

"All right, well we need to eat," Bert says, stepping into the argument.

"Sure we do, have to feed our lord and masters," Enid mutters.

Acid burns its way up to my throat. I want to argue with them, I want to prove them all wrong, but I understand them better than I should. I was the outcast before. Always on the outside, disenfranchised with no say in my future. I feel their pain even if I don't agree with it.

Besides how do I argue with them any better than Mei did?

They're not wrong. Mei isn't wrong either. This is just about the stupidest time to be looking at elections or fairness. I don't know the counts but I'm sure more than half the approximate three hundred survivors are not taking epis. Those not taking it are heading into the extreme limits of being dehydrated. They're sick, they can't work, putting the burden for their care on those of us who can. I've even heard there have been deaths. You can't take enough water to fight against the heat of Tajss. The cool evenings are over thirty-eight degrees Celsius when the suns are down. It's much hotter when the dual suns are in the sky. Human bodies aren't designed for this.

Mei comes over to my table and takes up the meat I've butchered then wraps it. Turmoil dances in her eyes. An ache in my chest makes me want to comfort her somehow. She's a good person, trying to do the right thing. Her hands shake as she tries to wrap the meat. Tears form in the corner of her eyes. She fumbles with the wrapping until I place my hand on hers. She looks up and I smile. Her smile is tentative, shaky, so I grasp her hand. She takes a deep breath then shakes her head.

"Sorry," she says, speaking soft so only I can hear her.

"Why? You were amazing," I say.

She shakes her head, and a tear falls down her cheek. "Why don't they understand?"

I shrug. "They're scared."

Mei nods, pursing her lips. "Me too," she says, another tear dropping.

My stomach clenches tight, I can't get enough air. I don't care that everyone is looking, I walk around the table and wrap her in my arms. Enid and I lock eyes over Mei's shoulder. I glare, Mei doesn't deserve this. I don't care if they're mean to me but Mei is too damn nice.

"Sorry," she whispers as we step apart.

"You're fine, screw those bitches," I say, making sure I'm loud enough they hear.

They ignore me but Mei's eyes widen and her hand flies to her mouth. She makes a tentative glance over her shoulder then back. Flashing her my best grin I shrug. She stays at my station working the supplies with me and we pass the time with small talk. No one says much the rest of the afternoon until at long last we're done. All that work and it might keep us fed for four, maybe five days if we're lucky.

There are too many of us and not enough of us willing to go out and hunt. Calista is working on growing crops, botany was her specialty on the ship, but she says it will be months before she has anything viable and Jolie is too pregnant to help. Until then we're dependent on the fast diminishing supplies from the wrecked ship and the hunting parties.

"Are you coming to the common area tonight?" Mei asks as we walk outside.

Enid slips out behind her, trying to avoid a confrontation. The look on Mei's face makes it clear she doesn't want trouble either. Part of me wants to tell Enid off but the more rational part resists the urge.

"I might," I say, stretching and yawning. "I'm pretty tired so I might just crash."

"Okay, well, hope to see you there."

She holds her arms out and I step into her embrace then she walks off. Walking alone to my apartment I roll my shoulders working the tension out. Butchering is hard work and as Bert pointed out, more than once, I'm not good at it. I try, damn it, but the damn knife never seems to go through the meat the way it does for him. I have to get better at hunting. One, I like it better, and two, if I'm hunting I won't have to butcher.

Astarot hasn't said anything about me yelping and infuriating the alpha bivo at our last kill. God that was embarrassing. I didn't expect there to be so much blood. Or it to be so hot. My stomach flips over at the memory. So gross but food on the table is worth it, right? Practice. I have to practice.

"Hey there," Astarot's voice sounds and I look up and around, my heart pounding.

He's leaning against the building five feet away. I don't know how a guy so big can move so damn quietly. I didn't know he was there!

"Uh, hey," I say, calming myself.

Astarot walks closer until he's filling my space. A hint of exotic, spicy musk fills my senses and my body responds. He's so big, strong, towering over me. He smiles as he leans in, coming closer to my lips.

"Hey, one night stand," I say, stepping back but he moves with me.

"Right," he says, as his lips touch mine.

I can't help myself, I return the kiss. His lips are amazing, magical in the way they move against mine. There's a taste to him, sweet and tart, enticing. His arms wrap around me, pulling me closer but I try to step back again.

"No," I shake my head. "I... we can't... I can't."

"Why not?" he asks, not backing up.

"Because..." I trail off.

It's hard to focus. He's so, there, imposing and my body is thrumming with desire for him. He was the best damn lay I've ever had, hands down. There's no denying that and my body wants more no matter what my brain and mouth are trying to say.

"Yes?" he asks, hands running over my ass.

"I don't want to... it's not permanent," I say.

"So you have said," he replies then resumes kissing his way across my cheek, down my neck.

"Astarot, we can't, I won't lead you on," I say, trying one

last time to step back.

Damn my body hates me, I'm wet, my nipples are rock hard. The cloth touching them hurts they're so tight. My panties are soaked. I want to let him have his way with me but I also don't want to hurt him. I care about him and I need him. He's my teacher. No one else will take the time to teach me to hunt. I need that so I can make my place in this new world.

"Fine," he says, stopping at last.

His eyes, those gorgeous, violet-purple eyes burn with passion. His huge cock bulges in his pants, leaving no doubt what he wants.

"Are you sure?" I ask, doubt in my voice.

He grins, shakes his head, then moves closer again. His cock presses into my abdomen, butterflies dance in my stomach.

"I'm sure I want you," he says.

My hands come up to his chest. He grabs my wrists and pulls them over my head, pushing me back until I'm pressed between him and the crumbling wall. Faintness washes over me, I can't think clearly, desire is a pounding need. His lips press into mine then his tongue, insistent, forces its way into my lips and I melt.

No man has ever handled me like this. He's dominant, forceful, yet gentle. He kisses me deeply, passionately, then steps back, grins and turns away.

"What?" I gasp.

"You said one night stand," he says over his shoulder, then he shrugs and walks away.

My body aches for his touch. I can't believe he's leaving me like this. It's a joke? Right?

He turns the corner and I wait, longer than I should, hoping he'll come back.

Have I screwed this up?

5

ASTAROT

"*A*gain," I order Lana.

Lana glares, grimaces, then climbs back to her feet. As she bends to pick up her stick, I can't help but admire the view of her full, round ass. She adjusts her grip, turns, then drops into a defensive stance.

I attack, pressing her hard. She blocks one, two, then a third blow, but she stretches out for that one. I swing my staff around and sweep her feet out from under her.

"Ugh," she grunts hitting the ground. "Damn it!"

Reaching out my hand to her, she stares at it, then ignoring my offer of help climbs to her feet. She picks up her staff, adjusts her grip, and drops into a defensive stance. Damn it, is right. Things are different. I should have known better.

"Again," I say.

She attacks, this time taking me by surprise. Her staff is a flurry of motion. The clack of wood is loud in my ears as our staves meet. The strange, human habit of excreting moisture happens as beads form on her head when her brow furrows in concentration. She forces me back. I swing my tail, trying to surprise her, but she leaps up and over, landing on her feet while swinging her staff around at my middle. The move surprises me and she lands a solid blow.

"Ughff," I exclaim as the wood connects with my ribs.

Lana smiles, for the first time today, and the sting disappears.

"And that is how you handle a stick," she quips.

"Great," I say, rubbing my ribs.

As we stand looking at each other the moment stretches. My cock stirs to life.

"Let's go again," she says, stepping back and breaking the moment.

I nod agreement though I feel anything but. I want to talk to her, tell her how I feel. How much I want her, no, how much I need her. Emptiness pounds inside me and I know she's the one to fill it. When I'm with her, I feel complete. Alone, in my bed at night, I'm lost without her.

She's pressing me hard, again. It's good because it forces me to focus, push aside thought. I have to be in the moment. Watching her move, the shift of her hands, where her eyes are, she drops her left shoulder, just a little but I see it and prepare. In a quick move she shifts her grip on the staff and swings it overhanded trying to come down on my head. I raise my staff with both hands and catch her blow.

I step in as a I catch it. We're close, so close I can smell the hint of something minty on her breath, the sweet smell of her sweat. Our eyes lock, something flashes in hers, sparkling as a grin forms in her face.

"Nice move," she says.

"Thank you," I say.

I'm drawn in by her, closer, the barest space separates our lips. It will be all right, just a touch, something to get me by. She doesn't move back but doesn't welcome me in. I stop, knowing this is a mistake. I step back.

"Again?" she asks, as the tension drops.

Pursing my lips my mind races through possibilities.

"I have an idea," I say.

"Oh?" she says, dropping her staff from guard.

"Go hunting with me, just you and me, a few days in the wild. I'll teach you more about how to survive."

Her eyes light up as a smile spreads across her face from ear to ear. "Are you serious?"

My throat closes seeing her excitement, unable to speak I nod. Dropping her staff, she throws herself into my arms. Her lips crush against mine, my cock jumps and I lift her off her feet. I never want to let her go. Her in my arms is all I'll ever need.

"This is great, what do we need? Who do we need to tell, I know, I'll tell Rosalind. She'll okay it, we need more meat and supplies."

Words flow out of her so fast I can barely keep up. She makes plans for an expedition without my input. Her face shines with joy and a warm glow radiates from my core. I nod along with her then she runs, I have to stretch my longer legs to keep up.

It takes a couple of hours before we're ready to leave. Her excitement hasn't diminished in the slightest and it's infectious. My scales tingle with anticipation, at last, we'll be alone. While I have an ulterior motive to this trip, I will teach her how to survive. Unlike most of her race, she's open to learning. She doesn't filter everything through her hatred of my home like the others do; her interest is pure and beautiful.

Lana bounces from one foot to the other, rolls her shoulders to adjust her pack, and shifts her staff from hand to hand. The grin hasn't left her face. Rosalind is waiting with her. The human female alpha is tall, dressed in her clean white outfit that flows around her body. When she moves, it's as if she walks in a cloud. Her long, dark hair falls past her shoulders and her regal face projects an aura of command.

I like Rosalind. She's strong and in control. I admire her strength. Rosalind puts her hand out as I approach which I take in the human gesture of greeting. We clasp each other's wrists and nod.

"Astarot."

"Rosalind," I smile.

"Are you sure this is a good idea?" she asks, cutting straight to the chase, another trait I like about her.

"As good as any," I shrug. "We need food. The supplies are dwindling fast."

"Right but sending just two of you out there? It's not bad enough that the entire planet is a death trap ready to kill you for the slightest mistake, there are still the pirates too."

Tightening my jaw I nod my understanding. The pirates, who not only crashed the humans' ship here, but have terrorized my race for all of my memory. Slavers, we call them Zzlo. I haven't seen signs of them since the devastation, but that could be just because those of us who survived didn't talk to each other. Or maybe they weren't interested in a small handful of Zmaj. Before the devastation they would raid smaller villages and towns, taking the able bodied and selling them for profit.

"Yes, they are a concern," I agree.

"It doesn't matter, the whole point is to learn to survive," Lana interjects.

"The whole point is to not lose any of the few assets we have," Rosalind counters.

Lana's face flushes red as her mouth snaps shut.

"I understand, Rosalind. You're right, but if there are not more hunters, capable hunters, then we will not survive. The food supply will not fill itself and there are only a handful of Zmaj. We cannot provide for this many."

Rosalind purses her lips and I see the wheels turning behind those sharp eyes of hers. She knows I'm right but isn't ready to concede the point. Lana looks between the two of us biting her lower lip, waiting.

"So what are you thinking, long term?" Rosalind asks at last.

"That we need more hunters," I say, but it's obvious this doesn't answer her question. "If I can train Lana to hunt on her own, she can then lead her own party. If we can train a handful, over time, who can hunt on their own and lead their own parties-"

"We end up with a surplus," Rosalind cuts me off nodding. "Okay, I get it and you're not wrong."

"Thank you," I say.

"Remember this Astarot," she says, serious. "As you said, there are not enough Zmaj. We cannot survive on this planet without you. I can't afford to lose you anymore than I want to lose her."

I nod my understanding. Rosalind holds her hand out and once more we grasp wrists. Lana grins over Rosalind's shoulder.

"Four days," I tell her. "If we're not back in four days, something is wrong."

"Okay," Rosalind says. "Don't be late."

The airlock of the dome over the city makes a swooshing sound even as Rosalind speaks. Lana will not give her a chance to change her mind.

Together we head out into the desert. The heat rises as we step into the airlock. When the outer door opens warm wind blasts us with sand.

"Damn it," Lana curses, wiping at her eyes.

My outer lids closed before the sand could affect me but

she has no such response. She stumbles as we exit the airlock, bumping into the outer wall. Taking her by the shoulder I guide her out, then touching her chin I lean her head back so I can look. Leaning in to see her eyes brings our lips so close mine tingle. Her lips are full, pouty, ready for mine.

No, push that aside.

"I'm fine," Lana says, shaking her head as she wipes her eyes on last time.

She steps back from me.

"Okay," I say.

"Which way?" she asks.

"I thought we'd go to an oasis I know of," I say. "There is much to learn in the oases of Tajss."

"Great!" she says and we're off.

Rolling dunes of sand cast in striations of red, white, and tans surround the city. I lead us around the dome. We've come out on the northern side. The oasis I want to lead us to is southwest of the city. The humans shipwreck is in this direction as well and while I know there were pirates there, Shidan and Amara had a run in with them, which I hope has kept them from this area. Sverre spotted them operating to the northwest of the city before that where we left them unmolested. It's a guess and a chance but without more information there's not any other way to proceed.

"Damn, this is hard," Lana says. We've been walking for two hours and are making slower progress than I'd planned for. "I need wings like you."

"It would help," I say, folding my wings in.

"Ugh, okay, there has to be a better way than this," she says, fighting her way out up the dune we're climbing.

I hold my hand out to help her. She stares at it, frowning, then shakes her head.

"It's okay," I say.

"No, it's not," she counters. "If I will hunt on my own, I can't depend on you or any other Zmaj."

"You won't be on your own," I observe.

"You know what I mean!" she snaps.

Beads of moisture run down her face which is flushed red. Gritting her teeth, she pulls her left foot out from the loose sand it has sunken into and places it back down but it doesn't matter. Her foot sinks in to halfway up her calf. She repeats the same steps with her other leg but I can see the effort is exhausting her. Despite my bigger size, my wings and tail make travel across the loose sand easy. My wings lighten my weight, my tail guides, and I can move along the top of the sand spending minimal effort. Zmaj wings won't allow us to fly but they're ideal for traveling on Tajss.

"I need a break," she says as we reach the top of the dune.

She pulls out her water bottle, takes a long sip, then digs through her pack until she finds the epis. Tearing a small piece of the plant off she chews on it while she stares out across the desert, deep in thought. Dazzling beams of light dance across the rolling dunes as the suns continue their passage across the sky. It's beautiful, but it doesn't compare to Lana. The button up shirt she wears stretches tight across the mounds of her chest. I love the lines of her form. The curve of her side as it swells out to her hips, the way it curves back in down to her perfect feet.

Everything about her is stunning. My hearts skip every other beat while I lose myself in dreams of being with her once more but not in her foreign idea of a 'one-night stand'. I want her in a proper way. Forever. The Zmaj way. I know she's the one. We are meant, one for another. I know this with the same certainty I know the suns will rise in the morning. It is. There is no question.

She finishes chewing the epis then takes another drink of water. Wiping the moisture from her brow she turns, picks up her pack and settles it onto her shoulder, then grabs her staff. Turning she arches an eyebrow. Words being unnecessary we resume our hike.

I offer my help to her many times. As the day grows longer, she takes my offer more often. The strain is wearing on her. I admire her perseverance. The suns are low on the horizon when I see the outline of the oasis in the distance. The massive baoba trees stretch high on the horizon calling us forward. An oasis is a dangerous place while also being vital to any hunter. It is a source of water and it brings to it most of the wildlife of Tajss.

"Do you see it?" I ask, when we break.

"Huh?" Lana pants, she's bent over and resting her hands on her knees.

"The oasis," I say, pointing into the distance.

She straightens and shields her eyes with her hands. Her brow furrows in concentration, creating an adorable wrinkle between her eyebrows. She drops her hands to her side shaking her head.

"No," she says, frowning. "Maybe. There's a shadow on the horizon, it's all I see."

"That is it," I assure her. "It's not far now, maybe an hour."

"It will be dark by the time we get there," she says, wiping the moisture from her face again.

"Yes," I agree.

She sighs as she shifts the pack on her back. "Okay, let's do this."

She walks then I feel it.

"Stop!" I hiss, my voice low.

She turns around, throwing her hands in the air. "Stop? Why?" she says, too loudly.

The ground rumbles beneath us. A few hundred yards behind her the sand shifts, vibrating, a line of shaking sand turns towards her. My stomach clenches tight. Lana shakes her head as she turns again to continue walking.

"No," I hiss, reaching for her.

"What?" she shouts.

The rumbling increases, vibrating my bones. The line of shifting sand comes straight for her. Watching her eyes widen, she looks down, her jaw dropping. She looks up, meets my eyes then she's thrown into the air as the ground beneath her explodes up and out.

6

LANA

I'm flying. No clue what the hell is going on but I'm flying. I left my stomach behind on the ground where I was just standing. Astarot was telling me to stop and stand still. It irritated the hell out of me because I'm hot and tired. I want to get where we're going so I can lie down. Now this.

Something screams, a screeching sound ripping at my ears. I spin head over heel then I'm looking at the ground. Everything freezes as I stare down. This will hurt. My mind races through possibilities. How can I get out of this? Is there anyway that this won't hurt like hell? A hundred then a thousand ideas come and go. After the last one leaves on thing is clear, I'm screwed. I take a deep breath, pull my legs up to my chest, tuck my head and then time speeds up.

I hit the ground hard, knocking my breath out as I crash. I can't get in air. Inhaling does nothing. My lungs scream in desperation, unable to take back the oxygen they need. Something pops in my back. Pain explodes throughout my body in a flash of white, overriding the desperate need to breathe.

Somehow I feel separate from my body. I know I'm in trouble but a cool, calm sensation falls over me, like it's happening to someone else instead of me. A story I'm reading but not feeling. Strange. Sand, sky, sand, sky as I tumble away from where I was standing. Life was good over there, what the hell happened? I slam into a boulder protruding from the sand. It hurts like hell but it also knocks sense back into my lungs. Air pours in, relieving the burning. A trade off I suppose, the blinding pain of impact lessened in my gratitude of inhaling.

I'm hurt, but not bad. I don't think anything broke though I'll have bruises all to hell and back. Okay, next. As a hunter, this is the life I'm choosing. What would Astarot do? Get to you feet girl!

Good idea. My hands sink into the loose hand as I work my way to my knees.

My heart stops when I look and see what it is, a zemlja. One of the single most dangerous creatures on a planet filled with plants and animals all of which are trying to kill you. The zemlja make Tajss special, or did before the great war that devastated it.

The zemlja rises fifteen feet out of the ground, waving its long, worm-like body back and forth as it screeches. Thick, protective scales cover its body. Zemlja hunt by sound and vibration, traveling under the ground like an earthworm, leaving massive tunnels in their wake as they traverse the planet in constant motion. Where they travel is where the epis grows. The secretions they leave behind are necessary for its growth.

Astarot crouches a few feet in front of it on the dune. He looks over and shakes his head. I stop moving. Now I understand. Stupid, stupid, stupid! I should have listened to him. The zemlja swings around from its hole in the ground. The eyeless head that is nothing more than a mouth filled with rows of razor sharp teeth pointing in my direction.

I stop breathing in fear as much as a desire to make no noise. The muscles in my arms quiver. A tear slides down my cheek as it looks at me then rises back up in the air and swings a full circle. Slowly it lowers itself below the ground until it disappears leaving only a dark hole where it was. The ground rumbles, ever so slightly, as it travels away.

I'm still too scared to breathe. I don't move, Astarot doesn't move either. We're frozen in place staring at each other, waiting. I don't know how long we remain before at last he rises. His wings spread and he leaps into the air, gliding over to land in front of me. He grabs me from the ground and wraps me in his massive, strong arms.

I gasp, shudder, then the tears I've been holding back overtake me. Relief opens the floodgates of barely contained emotions. He grips me tight as I cry on his shoulder, wrapping my arms around him. Holding me tight, he doesn't say a word; he doesn't have to. In his arms, I'm safe. I've never been more grateful to someone else since my adopted mother.

"I'm sorry," I say, my voice cracking.

"It's fine," he says, his voice full of reassurance, without a hint of incrimination.

"I should have listen-"

He grabs my shoulders and forces me back until he meets my eyes, cutting me off.

"No," he says. "Do not do that. That is not the way of a hunter. Regret will bring you nothing but block learning. What can we learn from this?"

Drawing in a long, shaky breath, I clear my thoughts. What can I learn?

"Listen to you," I say.

"More," he says, insistent. "What if I am not there?"

A strange emptiness fills my core as I look at that idea.

Astarot not there? Strange, it was my idea, I'm the one who sold the idea to Rosalind, but I didn't think about it. It was just an idea that made sense without thinking of the reality. I don't like the idea of him not being there. Still, he's right. I'm here to learn, I must open my mind, find the lesson he is trying to teach.

I replay the incident again. Trying to pay attention to every detail. Find the things I didn't notice when it was happening. There! A vibration. I felt it but I ignored it. It was slight, subtle, but it was there.

"The vibration," I say, awe in my voice at my insight.

"Yessssss!" he says, his excitement drawing the S out into a hiss.

Pride swells my heart. His smile is like a beam of bliss. I've never felt more alive.

"I felt it but I didn't pay attention, that was the sign that a zemlja was nearby."

"Good Lana. You must always be aware of all your senses are telling you. It will keep you alive if you learn to trust in them and hone your instincts."

My hand is on his cheek. The rough edges of his scales tease my fingertips as I slide my hand forward. The scales tint a greenish color at the edges under my touch. Rising onto my toes my lips find his and we kiss. His cock stiffens, digging into my abdomen, but I'm not doing that here. This is a fling. That's all. He's my mentor, it's a mistake to confuse our relationship. He can't be my teacher and my lover both. As a lover he'd want to protect me, hide me away, like the other Zmaj treat their mates. I want more than that, need more than that. I'm finding my place in this world. A place where I belong, nothing can stop that.

Our lips smack as we part. Lights dance in his eyes. The moment stretches between us and part of me knows. I want more, he wants more, but no. Not now and not like this.

Keep it simple. I have to find a balance. Taking my hand from his face I look around and spot my pack where it flew off. Retrieving it, I spot my staff and get that. I can feel Astarot's stare as I gather my stuff. He doesn't say a word but I know.

"Shall we go?" I ask, smiling as I push past the awkwardness of words unspoken.

"Yes," he says, grabbing his own pack as we resume our hike.

It isn't much longer before I can see the outlines of the oasis myself. I wish I had his sight but my eyes just aren't as keen. The dual red suns have dropped below the horizon. Shadows stretch long as the final beams of light drop away. The air cools, well cool for Tajss which is still several degrees higher than my body would tolerate without the effects of the epis. When the trees of the oasis are a couple hundred yards away Astarot stops. Crouching down, he motions that I should do the same.

"The oasis is very dangerous," he says. "It is also a source of life. There is water, food, and shelter. There are also predators of many varieties. Some whom make their home there, some who pass through for the water. You should always be cautious in approaching an oasis. Do not walk in blindly."

"Okay," I say, nodding my understanding.

"Good," he smiles. "Let's find shelter for the night."

Trees tower over us as we get closer, casting even longer shadows. The stars are shining, working with the moon to cast a silvery glow across the landscape and outline the trees giving them an eerie presence. I move closer to Astarot before I even realize I've done it.

We stop just outside the line of the trees. The baoba trees have massive bulbous trunks that rise twenty to thirty feet before they branch out with wide leaves. Smooth bark covers the tree's base and a marvel to behold here on Tajss something that resembles grass grows around them. Well if grass was an intense yellow-ish color.

Astarot approaches the tree, inspecting it. I stay to his left and a step behind, watching what he does but not understanding yet. I've learned enough to not speak. He'll explain when he's ready. He runs his hands up and down the tree as we move a circle around it, then he checks the next tree over the same way before nodding in satisfaction.

"Majmum make their homes in the tree tops," he explains.

"What is a majmun?" I ask.

"Pack animals, primates," he explains. "Very dangerous, especially in a group which they almost always are."

"Ah," I say. "How do I avoid them?"

"Watch for claw marks on the trees," he says, running his hand over the tree closest to us.

"Got it, no claw marks."

"We need a shelter," he says, bending down and picking up a long branch that must have fallen from the tree high above. "Gather ones like this, do not go too far from me."

Gathering sticks isn't glamorous but I'm not here for glamour. This is my calling and even this simple, mindless task I take seriously. Each one I pick up, I test it against the one he showed me. Astarot grabs my arm by the wrist as I'm reaching for a stick, surprising me.

"Wha-" he cuts me off with a finger to my lips, staring down at the ground.

Something slides away from the branch I was about to grab.

"Careful," he says, letting go of my wrist.

Damn, I thought I was being careful. Nodding my understanding I kick the branch with my shoe before adding it to the growing pile in my other arm. Piling our sticks together Astarot sets to work. He shows me how to drive the longer sticks into the ground, leaning them towards each other, creating a framework. Then we gather the huge leaves that have fallen from the baoba and weave them through the framework. It doesn't take long before we're standing in front of a small shelter.

"Wow," I say, impressed.

"It will keep you out of the elements, but more the leaves will cover over your scent. Sismis and other creatures hunt by smell so it offers protection from that too."

I'm having a hard time keeping my eyes open I'm so tired. Excitement and adrenaline are the only thing keeping me going. Astarot and I stand close enough we're touching, looking over the shelter we built together. His hip brushes mine and out of nowhere I'm horny. Overwhelming, all consuming, I need to get off and bad. Tiredness forgotten I turn into him, rising on my toes.

Leaning in as our lips come together my large tits press hard into him. My nipples respond to the pressure almost painfully. His lips press into mine and I drive my tongue into his mouth. I don't want gentle, I want him to take me. His hands run over my ass, softly squeezing, but I want him to dominate me, hold me down and fuck me hard.

Grabbing his hard cock that is pressing into my stomach, I grip it tight and stroke. He groans into our kiss so I stroke faster. His dick swells, spasming in my hand. I don't ease my pressure, he has another to satisfy my need, I want him to lose control. Breaking the kiss and keeping my grip on his cock I use my other hand to free the fasten of his pants. I let go long enough for the pants to drop and his gorgeous, massive cock springs free.

I take it in both my hands and stroke, focusing on the soft, unprotected underside. Lowering myself to my knees I tease the head of his dick with my tongue. Unfastening my shirt I work my clothing to free my breasts while pleasuring his cock. His hands twine in my hair, pulling, causing me to groan.

"Yes!" I encourage him.

That's what I need. I take more of his cock in my mouth. Lavishing him with my tongue, stroking the shaft, my free hand teases my nipples, moving back and forth. My panties are soaked, my nipples are hard tips I pinch and pull as I slide his cock in and out of my mouth.

"Lana," he hisses my name, and it drives me wild.

My hand slides across my stomach and into my pants, feeling my wetness. His cock swells, jumping in my mouth, his grip in my hair tightens and he pulls me forward. The fire burning in my core flames higher. Sliding a finger into my soft folds, penetrating them until I graze my clit. Pleasure explodes through my body, blinding, white burning through my nerves.

He's pushing me on and off his cock with his tight grip in my hair. It's just on the edge of painful and exactly what I want and need. I take his cock deeper with each forward push until it's bumping the back of my throat. Working my clit with my fingers pleasure builds as I take him deep.

"Fuck me," I say, pulling back from his cock.

He doesn't hesitate. Grabbing me up into his arms he holds me up as if I weigh nothing then impales me on his massive, ridged cock. It slides into my wetness easily, much easier than before. I'm ready for it. He fills me completely, pushing my body to its limits then just beyond. I throw my head back, crying out my pleasure as he bottoms out inside me.

He doesn't stop, it's not enough. Wrapping my arms around his neck to hold myself up, he puts his hands on my ass and then bounces me up and down. I ride his cock. Each thrust drives down until the hard ridge on his pelvis is rubbing against my clit sending new waves of overwhelming pleasure burning through me.

He pulls me up until just the tip of his dick is inside my wetness. Gravity pulls me back down then I'm up. He raises one hand, lifting me up and down with the other, twining it in my hair. He jerks my head back and licks my neck up to my jaw then down.

"Yes!" I scream. "Fuck me Astarot."

I'm going to explode. There is no way to contain this much pleasure. White lightning runs through me, burning new pathways, schooling my body in pleasure.

"Yes, yes, yes," I pant.

"Lana!" he cries out, driving deep inside then holding.

He throws his head back, a wordless hiss that goes on and on. Adding my groan to it I'm taken by my orgasm. It rips out from my core. Shuddering, muscles clench and unclench until, slowly, it passes and I collapse back into him.

Breathing heavy, neither of us move. I rest my head on his shoulder, trying to catch my breath while I wait for my heartbeat to slow and return to normal. His cock softens inside me, still massive, bigger than any human cock.

Kissing his neck I work my way up to his ear and nibble. A shudder runs through him and he laughs, moving away. He's sensitive after he comes, I note smiling. I kiss across his jaw finding his lips. Gentle, soft kisses, with my legs wrapped around his waist and our bodies melded together.

Something nags at my attention. Astarot's grip around my waist tightens and he pulls away from my kiss.

"What is it?" I ask.

He shakes his head and makes a shushing noise. A sound. Something off, I can't put my finger on it. It's not the normal quiet of the desert. A machine!

"What?" I whisper.

Astarot lifts me off of him and sets me on my feet, pulling

his pants up and grabbing his lochaber. He puts a finger to his lips as the sound grows louder. It's some kind of machine and it's coming closer.

"Pirates," I whisper, my stomach sinking as the icy grip of fear closes around my heart.

7

ASTAROT

*T*ightening my grip on my lochaber I nod. It has to be Zzlo. There is no other possibility. The whine of the strange machine grows louder. There is nowhere here to hide and I know the Zzlo work in groups. We can't fight them, they'd outnumber us, even if Lana was a more capable fighter.

"What do we do?" she whispers.

My bijass rises; that primal instinct that reduces everything to black and white. Survival is all to the bijass. The urge to protect her, my mate, my treasure is overwhelming. It urges towards destruction. Take any threat head on.

No. Smart, I have to be smarter than that. I can't take on an entire Zzlo patrol alone. Shidan tried that, and it didn't go in his favor. If they're coming to the oasis, then we need to not be here. Even if they're not, the oasis is a landmark. It draws the eye and they will see us

"Follow me," I whisper, I know they couldn't hear us but it doesn't matter.

Taking her hand I hurry along the edge of the oasis looking out to see if I can spot the source of the sound.

Opening both my lenses to gather in more of the dim light I see a cloud of dust in the distance. We've got time, good.

Straight, to the north, is a rocky outcrop. If we have to fight, I will have higher ground but I hope to find a place to hide in there. If I was alone, I could hide in the sand but Lana does not have that ability. I don't know if she could survive hidden underneath the Tajss surface and won't risk it.

Glancing back, I realize she hasn't taken time to close her shirt. Her beautiful mounds bounce in the soft moonlight and my second cock stirs to life. The silvery light outlines the dark centers of her breasts, they bounce as we move, distracting and exciting me. She sees me staring, looks down, then grins.

"Now?" she asks, shaking her head but smiling.

"You're beautiful," I say, shrugging.

"Thank you," she says, but her face changes color as she looks away.

I want to find out what I said wrong but we don't have time. We have to get to safety. As we leave the cover of the oasis I crouch down, a quick glance and I see Lana is following suit. I don't want to create a profile against the emptiness. The sound of the engine grows louder as they close with us much faster than we can move. It's a low whine echoing across the sound that makes my scales itch.

The first outcroppings of rock rise around us. Slipping between two large ones I pull Lana behind me then stop to look for our possible pursuers. Lana crouches down behind the rock while I look around the side of it. The sound is louder and now it's close enough I can see the machine itself and not just the dust cloud that follows it.

It is a metallic, gray box that looks like it is floating just over the ground. Dust flies up from underneath and behind. It turns toward us. Gritting my teeth, I loosen my lochaber as I turn and look behind us. The rocks rise, reaching for the sky. The side is smooth, worn by the blowing sand. There are no handholds.

Well out of Lana's reach is a cliff. There are more outcroppings up there that would offer protection and hide her from sight. I grab her up without a word. She yelps in surprise as I lift her over my head but she's sharp. She grabs the edge and scrambles over. As I thought, once she's up there I can't see her from down here. Her head appears over the edge and she looks at me questioningly. She holds out a hand but I shake my head.

"Come up here," she whispers.

"Hide, I'll be fine," I say. "No matter what, hide."

"No, damn it Astarot."

Shaking my head, I turn my back on her and crouch down behind the rock, my lochaber at the ready. Leaning over I watch the machine as it draws closer. My heart rate slows as a cold calm comes over me. The bijass comes like an old lover. Complexities drop away as it takes control. There is a beautiful simplicity in kill or be killed. I am a survivor, a hunter, and I will not lose.

The smooth shaft of my lochaber is cool as I adjust my grip. No matter how fast the box is coming, I see it moving in slow motion. My hearts beat slow, steady, and my breathing falls into time. My mind is clear, ready. Observing and preparing.

The box machine changes direction. I will it away. This is my territory, it is not welcome here. Leave or I will destroy you. It shifts further then it is moving away. I remain in my crouch waiting until only its dust trail is in sight. Rising I listen, in the distance a hunting Sismis screeches.

"Astarot," Lana says, her voice drifting down.

Turning I look up at my treasure. She's mine, it pulses in the core of my being. Mine. Her eyes widen, her mouth tightens into a hard line. Something is wrong. A tickle at the edge of awareness. Something... what is it? The fog of the bijass recedes. Shaking my head to clear it I look at her again.

"Are you... okay?" she asks.

I don't answer until the bijass has receded enough I feel in control again.

"Yes," I say, lifting my arms to bring her down.

She slides over the edge of the ledge into my arms. Lowering her down, her hands run across my chest. Desire stirs but it's late and we need to sleep. The sismis are hunting and I'd rather not fight more tonight. There is no reason to put her at risk. She stares into my eyes as if trying to find something.

"You're sure you're okay?" she repeats.

"Yes," I say, taking her hand and leading the way to our shelter.

"You looked... different, for a minute."

Part of me doesn't want to respond to that. I've hidden nothing from her before but this is hard. We walk in silence as I wrestle with what to say. Stepping into the cover of the oasis is a relief. The shelter we built is not far away. Once at it I stop and let her climb in first, then join her. We have to crawl in as it's built low and there's just enough room for two.

Lying with Lana's body molded to mine, my hand resting on her hip, the light scent of her hair in my nostrils, I confront what happened, giving control to the bijass is regrettable. It didn't take me by surprise or overwhelm me, I reverted to a primal state to protect her. There is no doubt in my mind, I'd do it again.

I WAKE WHEN SHE STIRS, ALERT AND READY IN AN INSTANT. MY senses strain for any hint of danger, searching for any threat.

She stretches then yawns loudly. Satisfied that we are in no danger, I slide out of the makeshift shelter and stand before stretching my own muscles.

Lana climbs out and reaches for the sky. The rising suns outline the curves of her body emblazoning her with a halo of fiery light. She rotates at her hips, stretching her back, but it thrusts the soft mounds of her chest forward in a bold way that makes it hard to focus my thoughts on anything else. Her hips circle, coming towards me and away, my cock pulses, hard and ready.

"Morning," Lana says, covering another yawn with her mouth. "Damn I'm stiff."

I turn away from her and look out over the oasis. If I spend any longer looking at her we'll get nothing done today. Even so I take a moment to clear my head and focus. We're out here so I can teach her, so what first? Healing salve is a basic, vital tool for survival. I'll teach that first.

"Are you hungry?" I ask, turning back to her now that my head is clear.

"Starving," she says.

She turns and bends over, reaching for her pack just inside the shelter. Her beautiful, curvy ass points at me and all the effort to clear my thoughts flee before an image of her naked before me on all fours. I close my eyes and breathe, listening to my hearts beat. Slow, steady, focus.

"You okay?" she asks.

"Yes," I answer, but I don't open my eyes until I'm sure I'm in control.

We sit beside our shelter and break our fast with pieces of guster meat and water. Once we've sated our hunger, she puts the food away in our packs.

"So, what's next?" she asks, vibrating with an excitement that is palpable.

"There is a healing salve, I want to teach you to make it," I say. "It's good for cuts, bruises, and muscle tears."

"Oh, yeah, Calista has mentioned that before," she replies. "Great! What do we have to do?"

Climbing to my feet I offer her my hand and help her to her own. "First, we kill a plant."

"Doesn't sound too hard," she says, frowning. I smile and shake my head. "Or I could be underestimating."

"It's wise to never underestimate an opponent, one of the first lessons I can teach you."

"Okay," she says, frowning as she considers.

"This way," I say, pointing deeper into the oasis.

"Bring our packs?"

"No, they should be fine here," I say. "If majmun were near, we would bring them. No other animals will dig through a pack like they will."

"Wow, okay," she says.

She takes up her staff and then we walk side by side, making our way between the huge tree trunks. The oasis is an island of sounds. Leaves rustle far overhead in a breeze we don't feel. Brush rustles as small creatures run from our approach. Lana moves with a practiced silence. Pride swells until it feels like I'm glowing with it.

She's sharp, learning fast, and listens to everything. She's moving as I taught her now, placing toe first then bringing her weight down after testing each step. When I first showed her this, she moved slow and awkward, but now she moves along quick and natural as if she's always walked this way.

Something makes my scales tingle so I hold up a fist. She stops at my signal, bringing her staff to a ready position. I don't know what I'm looking for but I know there's something. Long years of surviving have honed my instincts. I trust them and that has kept me alive.

Another sound, subtle, a slithering of something sliding

along the yellow grass and underbrush of fallen leaves and debris. Crouching down I turn a slow circle until I spot the subtle shift of a large, fallen leaf. Holding up a finger I circle it in the air making sure I have Lana's attention then point. She crouches and her eyes search where I'm pointing. Her eyes widen, mouth opens to an O, and she glances over at me questioning without words. I nod saying nothing until the movement stops. Rising I smile.

"That was a zmeya, a deadly poisonous snake."

"Oh, how did you know it was there?" she asks.

"The slithering sound," I reply. "Trust your ears and your instincts."

"Got it," she says.

Moving on, it isn't long before we are close to the heart of the oasis and I see my goal. A cvet, it's close to the base of a baoba tree where they grow so they can attract and capture small game. The cvet is big, with a bright orange-yellow middle with hints of red and its dark center is almost like a huge eye. They're hard to see from our position but pure white, almost clear, fronds grow across the colorful center. Those fronds contain a paralytic that will stop you cold. Green and brown leaves stretch out, wide and thick with vines between them that grow from the center. When I take a step closer the leaves tremble, it's aware of us.

"That is a cvet," I say, pointing.

"It's beautiful," she says.

"Yes and deadly," I agree, then explain the plan. "Follow my signals, we need its leaves."

I motion for her to move to the far side. When she nods her understanding we separate and move so we're opposite each other. I whirl my lochaber, positioning the blade over my head, ready to swipe down. I motion her forward and she advances with her staff at the ready.

The vines shift as she approaches, but she's prepared.

Swinging her staff around, she blocks the vines that move for her legs. They wrap around the staff. The cvet is not intelligent and will mistake the staff for the prey it seeks. I make my way closer while its attention is on her staff. I have to reach the center to kill it without being entangled in its vines or getting touched by the poisonous feelers.

"Ah!" Lana cries out.

The cvet jerks her forward. She didn't let go of the staff in time. In slow motion I see her stumbling forward, being dragged along behind the staff, struggling to stay on her feet.

"Lana!" I yell, rushing in.

Vines spring to life around me, swinging wildly, slashing at the air. I slice them away with the blade of my lochaber, clearing my path forward.

"Help!" she cries out.

"Let go!"

"I can't!" she says, then I see that the vines locked her hands to the staff.

The cvet trembles, shaking all over. Vines shoot out at me, trying to get around my legs. I have to stop and fight them off, losing precious seconds. Lana is being drug into the waiting mouth of the cvet. She screams, fear in her voice. My hearts pound in my chest, hard and loud, my muscles thrum as adrenaline pumps through me. The bijass swells, pushing in and vying for control.

Cutting through the vines I step forward, but my foot comes down on one of the cvet's large leaves. It pulls out from under me and I lose my footing. I'm jerked up and over, landing hard on my back. The air knocks out of me as I hear Lana scream once more.

8

LANA

*D*amn it, not again! I berate myself.

It moved faster than I expected. The vines didn't just wrap around the staff like Astarot said but caught my hands too. It was faster than I could blink. How the hell does a plant move so fast?

Digging my heels in, I try to stop the forward motion. My feet slip on the grass unable to find purchase. There's a scent on the air that reminds me of something gone foul, like bad meat. The closer I'm drug to the core of the plant the worse it gets. Cold chills run up my spine and down my arms.

Astarot is coming, but I don't want him to have to save me. If I'm to be a hunter I need to survive on my own. The vines wrapped around my wrists are tight, making my hands numb. I can flex my fingers and that's it. Leaning back, I throw my weight against the forward motion. I slow but can't stop.

The long, thick leaves of the plant surround me, each of them vibrating. They're slick and impossible to find traction on. I'm almost to the center of the plant. At a distance it was beautiful, this close it's terrifying. The center which looked like it was colored black from far away, is actually a mouth with teeth! It's also the source of the smell which is now overwhelming. The odor burns my nostrils making my sinuses hurt.

"Astarot!" I cry, looking up for him.

He's using his blade to cut his way towards me but something happens and he flies up into the air and slams down on his back. He hits so hard I feel the impact in my bones. The vines around him rise into the air, waving in some kind of weird victory dance. His blade flashes, reflecting the sun's light as he whirls it.

The vines gripping my wrist loosen when he cuts through. Jerking my hands free, I grab my staff as it falls to the ground. Twirling it up and over my head, I shift my grip then bring it down overhand to slam it onto the main body of the cvet. It shudders, the ugly hole of a mouth closes then opens again. It's not the effect I was hoping for but better than nothing I guess.

Whirling my staff once more I bring it next to my side and thrust forward, using it like a spear. The stabbing motion pokes into the orange-red center which gives under my thrust feeling soft and mossy. It doesn't appear to do any permanent damage so still not effective, damn it.

Something shifts under my feet then I lose my balance and slam onto my back. Stars fill my vision as I gasp for air. Vines wave in the air over me. Raising the staff I use it as a shield while scrambling backwards. The vines show no interest in me as I'm able to scramble back from their immediate reach. Climbing to my feet I see why.

Astarot is on his feet again. He wields his lochaber with deadly accuracy. The lochaber is a staff, not unlike mine, but is has a long, curved blade on one side. The blade is slicing through the cvet's leaves and vines like they're nothing. Astarot leaps into the air, his wings spreading wide, he hisses loudly. Gliding forward on the power of his jump, his tail swings to guide him as he whirls the lochaber around. The point of the blade faces down as he slams into the center of the cvet.

Gore sprays out coating both of us. The vines and leaves drop lifeless to the ground. The entire thing shudders then lies still. Astarot pulls the lochaber free, wipes gore from his eyes, then turns around.

"Are you okay?" he asks, jumping down.

"Yeah, I'm fine," I say, my cheeks warm with embarrassment. "Sorry, I screwed it up."

"You did good."

"Sure," I shrug.

His hands cup my chin, tugging until I look up at him. Tears well in my eyes as my stomach clenches. I tighten my jaw trying to not cry.

"I mean it," he says.

Closing my eyes I breathe deep. This is all I want, to find my place in the world. I want to be useful, to have a purpose. I know I can do this. Swallowing, I nod, waiting for my throat to open so I can speak again.

"Thank you," I say, my voice hoarse. "I need to be better."

"And you will be," he says, his confidence cuts through the emotions and upset. "Now, pay attention. The entire point of this is to show you how to harvest the sap from its leaves."

He shows me how to slice the thick leaves then squeeze the sap out of them into small jars that we seal with treated leather and string. It takes quite a while but we fill five jars with sap before we're done. Once Astarot shows me the way to do it I do one on my own, making a mistake he has to correct. The next three I do without error. His broad smile fills me with pride.

"So," he says, glancing down at himself. "We should wash up then we'll start off again."

"Sounds good," I say. "What else do we need?"

"Sismis claws," he says. "Grind them up, add the powder to the sap, and you have a good healing salve."

We talk while making our way through the oasis. It's only a few minutes before we step into a clearing dominated by a beautiful, turquoise pool of water. Astarot peels his clothes off while walking into the water. I hesitate only for a moment before doing the same.

The warm water is almost hot and feels so good on my sore muscles. The grime and gore of the cvet rinses away and I feel more alive than I have in a while. I wade out until it's deep enough I can just touch the bottom by standing on my tiptoes. Astarot goes out further, his greater height allowing him to touch bottom longer, then he ducks under the water, disappearing from sight.

"Astarot?" I call out, turning a circle after a few moments.

No bubbles, no response. He must be messing with me. He has to be, right? Doubt niggles at the corner of my thoughts. He has to be fine. No signs of a struggle, there'd be a struggle, I'm sure of it. It's a joke.

Astarot bursts out of the water a foot in front of me with his wings spread wide and his arms held out. I throw myself back. I guess water games don't change between races. Laughing, he chases after me, slowed by the water. I dive in and swim away. In the water I'm quicker than he is, my smaller form giving me an advantage. We play and splash and laugh. It's fun and more normal than my life has ever been.

I'm diving away from him once more when he catches my leg by the ankle and pulls. I kick to break free but I know I don't stand a chance so I turn over onto my back and float. He pulls me in closer, spreading my legs to either side. Beneath the water his cock presses against my pussy.

He looks surprised when he realizes the position we're in.

He stops pulling me forward, purses his lips, and looks up. Our eyes lock and I see he's asking permission. Biting my lower lip I nod. I want him, bad. He slides into me easily to the first ridge of his dick. Once that hits my pelvis he pulls with an easy, steady pressure and I breathe.

His cock slides in, expanding my pussy as my body adjust to his girth. My eyes roll up in my head as he thrusts in. I've never felt anything better than him entering me, filling me to my limit. Once he's in he pulls me up by my arms until our lips meet. I wrap my arms around his neck and we move against each other, grinding.

We kiss and move, sweet, passionate love. An orgasm builds quick, taking me in its grip and holding me tight until I'm lost in the pleasure. When it passes from me he's holding me tight, letting my body relax.

He carries me out of the water and standing on the sand I ring my hair out then work it into a quick braid. Once I've finished that I'm dry enough to get dressed. Astarot is leaning against a tree watching.

"Enjoying yourself?" I ask.

"Very much," he smiles.

I laugh and shake my head. "I've had an idea."

"What about?"

"How to move across the desert," I reply. "I remember reading this story when I was young. It was about a boy who lived in this place called Alaska. It was all snow and impossible to walk on. He'd sink into it and not be able to move. So they used these wide shoes woven out of branches. It spread his weight which allowed him to walk on top of the snow. Seems like it should work for sand too, right?"

Astarot's brow furrows as he tilts his head to one side considering. He shrugs, holding his hands out in front of him.

"Maybe," he says. "Could always just grow you some wings."

"Oh yeah, let me get right on that."

"What? You'd look great with wings."

"You got an extra pair lying around?" I ask, arching an eyebrow at him.

"Nope, never have been good at sharing," he grins.

"Just as I suspected."

"What can I say?" he asks and we both laugh.

"I'd like to try my idea."

"Sure," he agrees. "What do you need?"

I sketch out the details of my idea for him. He gets the concept so we make our way back to the cvet. Using the side knife I carry, I harvest several of the leaves. I form a loose frame of fallen limbs and twine then cover the frame with the leaves. It doesn't take long before I'm fastening them onto my feet.

Staring down and admiring my work, joyfulness makes me feel light as a feather. Taking a few steps to test them, they seem to work. Nothing falls apart at least but I'm still on the grass of the oasis. The real test will be the sand.

"Ready?" he asks.

"Let's do this."

We walk out of the oasis and onto the open sand, holding my breath as I place my right foot down for the first time in my makeshift shoe. The sand shifts as I apply weight then stops. Smiling at Astarot I put my next foot forward repeating the process. I sink in but not as far as I do without the sand-shoes.

"Ha ha!" I laugh, pointing at my feet.

"Interesting," Astarot observes.

"That the best you got?" I ask, dancing from foot to foot putting weight on one foot then the other.

Astarot frowns, his forehead wrinkling as his brow comes

down, then he smiles.

"Amazing?" He makes it a question combined with a laugh.

"Better," I nod agreement, laughing with him. "Let's get moving."

"Can you carry your pack with those?" he asks, nodding at my shoes. "I will carry if for you."

"Thanks, but no, if they will work I need to test them in real conditions. I won't always have you there to carry my pack if I'm leading my team of hunters."

"Okay," he agrees, but the frown on his face tells his doubts.

"What?" I ask, shifting my pack on my shoulders as we walk.

"Nothing," he says, shrugging.

"Right, nothing, try again there buddy."

He looks away, staring over his left shoulder into the desert while avoiding my stare. Silence stretches out, is he going to answer me? What the hell is wrong with him? The conversation replays in my head but I don't see what the problem is.

"What?" I ask again. "Astarot, talk to me."

I can't keep the note of pleading out of my voice. I don't know what is wrong but the not knowing is eating at my insides like too much acid in my stomach.

"I hadn't thought of you being on your own," he says, glancing at me before turning away again.

My gut knots into a hard ball as my stomach muscles tighten, my heart constricts, and my throat closes tight. No one has ever said anything like that before. Never in my life have I felt wanted, needed, the emotion in his words makes my head spin. I don't know how to respond. I have to say something but words won't form.

"Oh," I say, at last more a sound than a word.

A tear falls so I turn away. I don't want him to misunderstand and I can't explain it, not now. We walk in silence, avoiding each other's gaze. Hadn't thought of me being alone. I've been alone my entire life. Unwanted by anyone but my adopted mother, but I was a drain on her. She never said so, did nothing outward, it was my observation. I'm not stupid and I saw what she sacrificed to save me. I love her for it but I never wanted to be what I was.

She gave up food, status, supplies, all so I could live. Never once did she even look at me with a hint of criticism. Never once with anything but love and adoration, but in my heart, deep inside, I knew her life would be better without me. As a doctor she had an exalted status on the ship, admired and respected, until me.

When she made the choice to keep me, adopt me and raise me, my vagrant nature made her less in everyone else's eyes. She was the one who went against the grain. Broke the rules, kept the unwanted. She never once showed any sign of regret for her decision. I loved her so much! Knowing I was the sole cause of her suffering was hard.

We've walked a long time, I'm not sure how long, spending the time lost in my own thoughts. The emotions Astarot stirred up ease and we resume our light banter, neither of us touching the subject that almost came up. About mid-day one of my sand-shoes snaps becoming a floppy mess.

"Damn it," I curse, stopping and unlacing it from my foot.

"Can you fix it?" he asks, kneeling down to inspect it with me.

"I don't think so," I say. "The branches just aren't strong enough and look, the leaves are losing their tenacity. It's been getting harder to walk with them for a while now. The idea is solid but the materials are not. I need something different, harder to make this work."

"I see."

Shaking my head, I unlace the other sand-shoe then store both of the prototypes on my pack. We resume our travels but without the makeshift shoes the going is much slower. We've been marching west for hours and now the open desert is giving way to rocky outcroppings. Growing larger in the distance it looks like a mountain range, or the Tajss equivalent of one. As if I'd know a mountain range that wasn't in a book. My entire life experience was on the generation ship.

Astarot helps me as we continue our journey and I take his help, grateful for it. Self-sufficiency is awesome, when it isn't also self-stupidity. I've done my best but I can't keep a good pace across the loose sand without his help. It isn't long before we're moving between huge boulders leading to the bigger rocks.

The boulders are twice as tall as Astarot on average. Weaving our way through them our vision is limited to the distance between us and the next one. It's almost like wandering through a strange maze. At least we have shade to cut the heat. I bump into Astarot's back.

"Wha-"

He places a hand over my mouth, cutting off my exclamation. Snapping my mouth shut I strain my ears and other senses as he's taught me. Something feels off now that I'm paying attention. Damn it, what did he say? I have to always be alert and paying attention to my instincts. The monotony of the trip lulled me into complacency.

Astarot reaches for the lochaber on his back just as I hear a grunt and then the clack of metal on metal. Three pirates step around the rock just in front of us, guns at the ready, aiming them at the two of us.

"Shit," I exhale, reaching for my staff.

9

ASTAROT

*S*creaming a wordless battle cry I leap for the nearest pirate. Surprise works to my advantage. Slamming into him with my body weight, I knock him back and into the other Zzlo behind him. The two stumble as they try to bring their weapons to bear. The third steps to one side, avoiding the impact.

Lana's staff swings next to me, hitting the third pirate in the head. The Zzlo pirates are ugly, their skin has an orange tint with a leathery look. Sharp teeth show as they make guttural sounds of surprise. Two spiky protrusions hang from either side of their mouths. The top of their heads are bald with black tentacles that pass for their hair around the sides. Gold and silver metallic bands decorate the strands at intervals down each one. They're wearing black leather outfits that serve as some kind of protective armor.

The one Lana hit stumbles back, reaching for his head at the point of impact. The two before me disentangle, retreating behind the rock using the tight quarters to their advantage. Grabbing Lana I throw her behind me. She cries out in surprise then grunts as her back slams against the stone of the rocky outcropping.

The third pirate raises his gun and fires just as I get my treasure safely shielded with my own body. Blue lightning jumps from the gun towards me. Time moves in slow motion. Instinct screams to dodge, move out of the way, but if I do, I leave Lana exposed. Instead I leap into it as the bijass rises like a dark cloud.

The lightning hits my chest, crackling as it spreads, burning. My muscles light on fire, overloaded nerves scream. My chest spasms then goes numb. I roar, spreading my wings to the width of the space, only about half their span. Flapping them hard I leap into the air, working them to force life back into the numb muscles of my chest and to help gain height in my leap.

The pirate tracks my rise with his weapon, his eyes narrow, his fists gripped to the shaft. I swing my tail beneath me and it slams into his chest, knocking him backwards. He hits a rock protrusion and grunts. Landing, I rush forward, leaning down to slam my shoulder into his solar plexus. Lifting as I make contact, I drive him hard into the rock.

The leathers he wears lessens the impact of his body but I knock his unprotected head into the rock. He grunts in surprise then slides down. An impact on my back steals sensation, causing my right side to go numb.

My right arm hangs useless, refusing to respond. Whirling as fast as I can, I'm struck again in the right side. Already numb it doesn't affect me as I charge towards the pirate who is firing, leading with my useless right arm and side.

Almost to him, two more steps, something moves to my left.

"Astarot!" Lana screams.

A glance is all it takes. The other pirate has her, a smaller weapon to her head. He grunts an order in his guttural language. Rage tries to take control. I'm struggling against losing myself to the bijass. I can't let him harm her.

My hesitation is too much. The other pirate fires, the turn of my body to see Lana was enough to expose myself. Blue lightning hits my left side, and it goes numb. Tingling pain absorbs both my limbs making them useless. They won't respond.

"LANA!" I scream at the top of my lungs.

My legs are working so I drive myself into the pirate. We stumble backwards on impact, but my arms won't react. I can't grasp him. Anger pulses, the dark cloud embraces more, I'm fighting the pirate and my need to remain in control. Giving over to the bijass is not an option.

He sweeps my feet out from under me. The ground flies up quickly then my face slams into it. A weight lands on the middle of my back, digging in as I'm held down. He forces my arms behind my back. The loud clack of metal fills my ears and I know I'm in chains.

I'm forced to my feet. The three Zzlo move together, talking in guttural clicks. One of them points at the first one I hit and makes a sound that can only be a laugh.

"Are you okay?" Lana asks, tears running down her face.

A bruise darkens her left cheek. The dark cloud surges up, focus!

"Yes, are you okay?"

She nods, biting her lower lip. They've bound her in chains too. The one the other two are making fun of lowers himself in front of me, working another set of chains. I kick him with all I've got. My foot contacts under his jaw. His head snaps back and blood flies from his mouth. Slamming my shoulder into the one on my left I swing my tail, trying to take the one on my right but he dodges.

Blue lightning hits me from two sides. Blinding pain. Can't think. Everything hurts. A sound. Lana.

"ASTAROT!"

She's screaming my name.

Kill them. They're hurting my treasure. Kill them all. Destroy them. I'll tear them apart. Bathe in their blood.

No!

Grabbing the dark cloud I force it back down, regaining control. Losing control is not the way. It won't free us or save Lana. No matter what I have to remain in control.

I can't move. My legs are numb now too. The pirates exchange more words then two of them hook their hands under my arms and drag. The third one leads the way with Lana in front, prodding her along with his gun.

They make their way through the maze of outcroppings. The painful tingling in my limbs increases as the numbness wears off. It's almost unbearable, and the bijass reacts to the pain, striving for control. It's call is tempting, there is no pain in the bijass, only rage. Primal instinct, kill or be killed.

I have to remind myself, over and over, that only intelligence will free us. Anything less will get us killed.

Emerging from the outcroppings in the same direction I was leading, one of their transports sits waiting. A large, dark gray steel box sits in stark contrast to the red and gold of the desert sand. Another pirate stands next to a ramp on the side that leads into darkness.

My limbs tingle, the pain is receding, but I give no sign that life is returning. I have to be smart, wait for an opportunity.

The pirates that captured us call out to the one waiting by the transport. He points at Lana then grabs his crotch making a thrusting gesture. The dark cloud rising comes tinted red. They laugh, building my rage further.

They will not touch her. I won't allow it.

I let my head loll side to side as if I'm still unaware. The pirates dragging me along drop me. Sand puffs up in my face, filling my nostrils. My filter lenses snap shut protecting my eyes. I'm turned so I can see the pirates. Shackles bind my arms behind me and another set are on my ankles. My tail and wings are free, giving me more of an advantage than they seem to realize.

The two that were dragging me disappear into the darkness of the transport leaving only two guarding us. The one waiting by the transport comes forward, his gun slapping against his middle, hanging from the strap around his neck. He's heading for Lana.

I can just see her at the edge of my vision. She stiffens as he approaches but gives no other sign of fear. Her eyes watch him approach, her mouth tightens into a hard line, but she stands straighter, confronting the threat before her.

Love and admiration of her incredible strength make me feel as if I might explode. The pirate closes with her, his hand reaches towards her face. She doesn't draw back. Darkness encloses my mind. Focus, push it back. Smart, have to be smart. Every fiber of my being wants to rip his arm off before his hand touches her soft skin. My skin. My female. My treasure.

He touches her face, tracing the line of her jaw. Lana leans into it and smiles. Anger rages in my heart, pounding through my veins. Mine!

Her smile grows wider. No, this can't be! Her leg swings up between his legs impacting him with a hard smack. He grunts in surprise, doubling over.

My treasure!

Lana spits at him as he straightens. He grabs her by her shirt, tearing it open and grabbing her breast. The bijass grabs me. There is no time to resist, it's there. Leaping to my feet, I roar, primal rage exploding.

The two pirates turn, shock on their faces. As they fumble for their guns, I slam into the one that dared to touch Lana. Raising my shoulder into him, I lift off the ground and throw him over my back. Spinning, my tail slams into the other one and I hear a satisfying crack of bone on impact.

He screams in pain, dropping to the ground. I'm facing the one I threw over my shoulder. He scrambles backwards, pushing with his legs, desperate to put distance between us.

Stalking forward I hiss, crouching over, my shackled hands reach for him. His gun rises, aiming, I leap. Landing on top of him his breath whooshes out. His foul breath rips across my face. Rising, lifting my arms over my head, gripping my hands together I slam down. I'll smash his head to pulp.

A sizzling white line wraps around my chest. Pain. So much pain. Can't think. It hurts. Everything hurts. My body shakes and spasms, uncontrolled. Eyes won't focus. Muscles won't respond. I'm trapped in a prison of my body.

It keeps going. No end. Too much pain. Can't fight it.

"ASTAROT!"

Lana's scream follows me into blackness.

LANA

S hit.

My wrists are numb, my arms ache, and I have to pee. The chain between my wrists hangs from a hook over my head, forcing my wrists to an odd angle. That numb, tingling feeling that isn't numb because how the hell can numb hurt so much?

Astarot lies in a hump across from me. They put more chains on him after his last attempt to protect me. Despite the situation, I can't help smiling. Protecting me. He did it all for me. He didn't react until one of them touched me then he exploded. He was a force of nature and if he wasn't taken by surprise, or had his weapon ready, I'm sure things would have ended differently.

Chills run through my limbs, I'm terrified, but the warm ball in my stomach helps. No one has ever stood up for me like that. My adopted mother protected me but her protection was quiet, reasoned. Astarot was like any hero in the movies I would sneak in and see when I could. He's like Wesley from *Princess Bride* but with rage.

I've never felt like this.

Now I have to save him. How strange is that? I've never had to worry about another person's survival. My own has always consumed all my thoughts. I will do whatever it takes for him. The transport has been humming and vibrating along for hours. We're traveling but to who knows where. Fear that Astarot has not woken or stirred in all this time rises but I push it aside.

Only one pirate is in the same section of the transport we are. He sits on a fold-out bench by a door that leads towards what I assume must be the front. It's time to put the skills that kept me alive growing up to use.

"Hey," I call.

He looks over and grunts, motioning with his gun.

Luckily he's the same one that was fondling me. That is something I know how to use to my advantage. The desire of men doesn't seem to change no matter how alien they are. Isn't that interesting?

"Hey," I say again, but this time I shift.

My torn shirt barely covers my left breast. My bra broke when I struggled to reach Astarot when they were hitting him with their electric whips. He was interested before, well here they are buddy.

His eyes lock on my cleavage. Perfect.

"I need a drink," I say.

His eyes dart up to mine then back to the exposed skin of my chest. Damn it, one track minds and a language barrier. Great.

"Come here!" I insist, making a come hither motion with my head.

He stands up, bracing himself on the wall as the transport bounces and shifts side to side. His eyes never leave my chest as he moves closer. He says something, or I assume it's words. Grunts and clicks is what I hear. I wait until he's close. He moves cautiously, staying out of the range of my legs.

"Can you let my arms down?" I ask, looking up at the chain that holds them above my head.

He looks up and shakes his head, grunting.

"Please?" I ask, shaking just enough to put a bounce in my full breasts.

I get the desired effect, his eyes drop back to my tits. Breathing heavy so that my chest rises and falls I purse my lips. Manipulation without going too far is a fine art.

"Please, my arms hurt," I say, which is not a lie.

He grunts, clicks, then shrugs his shoulders. I don't know if he understands my words, but he seems to at least get my point. I smile and shrug to put another bounce into my tits. He growls, grunts, then he moves in closer. My breath catches in my chest. The smell of him is disgusting. Like liver and onions with too much garlic thrown on top of it while smelling dirty too. Disgusting.

The chain holding my arms up comes loose then they drop. Relief rushes through me until it's followed by the pain of blood returning to my limbs. I didn't know it would be so bad! The pirate moves close, so close we're almost touching. My back is against the wall, I've got nowhere to go. Where would I run anyway?

Bracing myself, I smile at him. He's not as tall as Astarot but taller than I am. He's big, imposing, and there. A piece of me wants to panic, to scream like a maniac, or curl into a ball and hope it goes away. That's the stupid part. Behind the pirate is Astarot's still form, and it's all I need to feel brave.

Astarot needs me. After all he did to save me, this is the least I can do. I got this.

"Water?" I ask, miming a drink.

The pirate grunts and shakes his head.

"Please?" I ask. "I'm very thirsty."

Shaking his head, he pulls a container off his belt and

holds it out. I have to look it over before I figure out the opening. Once I do, I take a sip and spit it out. The pirate laughs in response to my spraying him with whatever the hell that was. It burns in my mouth, even after I spit it out. The little of it that touched my throat has caused a bonfire that isn't stopping.

It burns through my tongue traveling out across my limbs. It tastes awful but behind the burning is a renewed sense of vigor. I feel stronger, more alert, even more alive. Sniffing the container is regrettable. The scent is as strong as the burning that has yet to subside in my mouth. Tears stream down my face as my mouth rails against me for having inflicted this on it.

Good or bad, this is what Astarot needs. I take a step towards him then the pirate slams a hand down on my shoulder hard enough to bruise. His vice-like grip tightens, turning me around without option. When we're face to face, he shakes his head.

"He needs it," I say, all but begging. "Please!"

The pirate frowns, glances over his shoulder towards the door he was sitting by. I push forward, moving into him, smashing my breasts against his chest. His eyes widen. I look up into his beady, yellow eyes, pouting.

"Please," I say, breathless.

He lets go of my shoulder, shaking his head but freeing me. I don't worry about the mixed nature of the signal but move straight to Astarot. Kneeling next to him I run my hands over the cool scales of his face, turning his head so his mouth is facing up. I pour a small amount of the liquid into his mouth. Most of it pours back out but then he swallows. His body shudders, shakes, then his eyes open. He hisses as he jumps, trying to get to his feet.

He's too well bound. Chains clank and clatter as he shifts,

struggling against them. He glares at the pirate over my shoulder then leans back against the wall.

"Are you okay?" he asks, his eyes taking in my torn shirt, then staring at my face.

My cheek is swelling from the hit, I've got a dozen other bruises all of which hurt, but I can't be in as bad of shape as he is.

"I'm fine," I lie. "Are you okay?"

"I'll be fine," he says. "I'll get us out of here."

"I know," I smile, then a hand grips my shoulder and I'm thrown back onto my ass.

The pirate steps between the two of us grunting and pointing fiercely.

11

ASTAROT

*E*very part of me hurts but I don't care. Straining against the bonds, I'm able to force my way to my knees. The Zzlo between Lana and I backhands me across my face. I roll with the hit but blood flies from my mouth and splatters on the ground. A low, soft hiss slips out before I can stop it.

"I will kill you," I say, knowing full well he can't understand me but it doesn't matter.

He gets it that much is clear. He kicks me in the ribs. I'm lifted off the ground with the force. Something cracks, I feel it more than I hear it.

"Astarot, no!" Lana cries out. "Just wait, not yet."

She's right. I know she's right, now is not the time. I'll only lose. I need to find an advantage.

Letting my body go limp against the chains, I settle against the floor. The Zzlo kicks once more but doesn't put as much force into it as he did the first time. I grunt in pain then he leaves me alone. He grabs Lana by her shoulder and pushes her back to the opposite side of the transport. He doesn't fasten her back to the wall though, just pushes her into the seat then takes one next to a door at the far end of the space.

Lana and I look at each other. The space between us might as well be the length of an adult zemlja for all the good it does us to be so close. If my legs were free, I could stretch a foot over and touch her. Bound as I am, even my tail, I can't even come close.

"How long?" I ask.

"Huh?" Lana responds.

"How long have we been traveling?" I ask, wiping my mouth on my shoulder

"I'm not sure, seems like maybe five or six hours," she says, frowning. "Sorry, my time sense is crap."

I nod ignoring her self-doubts. Five or six hours. These machines travel fast, we would have reached Drakonov by now if that was their destination. Since they haven't stopped, it must not be. That's good, I guess. Though I have no idea where we're heading. We'll figure that out when we're free.

The Zzlo is watching us with squinty, suspicious eyes. I seem to have most of his attention but even so his eyes drift to Lana more than I like. The bijass dances around the edge of my consciousness, probing, waiting for an opportunity to take over. The metal floor and walls vibrate with a steady hum. One thing is for sure, we're moving further away from home. The only question remaining is can I get us free and then back.

My legs and wings are numb while my tail is a pulsing ache from the bindings. Every part of my body hurts from the beatings I've taken. Lana's head hangs down and when she looks up a tear trails down her face. My bijass rises again, pushing in, and I have to struggle with it.

The surrounding space is an empty box with chains clattering against the metal walls. It's obvious what the intended cargo is. The door next to the Zzlo slides open and another one looks in, grunting. Our guard rises, blocking my view into the next area. They exchange words then the door slides shut leaving only the guard.

When he turns around, he has a bag in his hands. He walks towards Lana who sits up, pulling at her shirt as she tries to keep herself from being exposed. Red rage pushes through me with every beating of my hearts. I hiss as I struggle to not lose control. The guard ignores me, moving so his back is to me while he faces Lana.

"What?" she asks.

I hear her but can't see past him.

He grunts in response and I see him move. It looks like he's waving something in front of her. The muscles of my arms and legs tense until it feels like they're about to explode. The chains clank as I strain to see what is happening to her. He grunts, more guttural sounds. Clenching my hands I can feel what his skin will be like when I close my hands around his throat.

"No," she says.

The bijass pushes in, no, I can't give in. Have to remain in control.

The Zzlo grunts, moving closer to her. Fight the rage, no, cannot give in. He can't touch her. She's mine. My treasure.

"Thank you," she says, then the Zzlo moves away and I see her.

The Zzlo moves back to his seat. Lana has the bag in her hand. She opens it and pulls out some cured meats from a container. Sitting down she nibbles on the meat then sips the drink. She doesn't look well, her eyes are sunken, her skin has a gray tint to it, unlike her normal color. Something is off, I have to get her out of here.

After a few minutes she stands up then braces herself against the wall before making her way across the space between us. The Zzlo watches her but doesn't react. Kneeling in front of me she holds a piece of meat up to my lips. She doesn't speak. When I don't open my mouth, she touches my cheek with her other hand. The Zzlo guard grunts, his voice loud, and rises to his feet. Lana jerks her hand back.

I take the meat and chew. Lana undoes the bottle and moves it towards my mouth but the guard is coming closer. His boots clang against the metal floor as he stomps over. His large hand clamps down on her shoulder tossing her backwards. Her eyes widen, her mouth drops open, and liquid flies out of the bottle splashing across the floor.

Lana slams down and I lose it. The bijass races in, muscles expand, rage burns through my veins. Something snaps and my hands come free. I grab the Zzlo, my legs, wings, and tail still bound so I pull him down. He cries out in surprise. Everything is red. Doubling my fists I slam them into his face. His head lolls to the side, blood flying out of his nose and mouth. He grunts in pain, raising his arms to protect his face. I pound into him over and over, no thought, only action.

Electricity crackles through the air and my back explodes into pain but I don't stop. I have to save my treasure. Somewhere distant Lana is screaming my name but I can't stop. He touched her, I must destroy him.

Pain. More pain. My back and legs are numb. Darkness edges the red rage of my view, closing in, but I can't let go. My hands are on his throat, squeezing. Flesh gives way, thumbs dig in as light fades. Gray fades to black.

"Astarot, no!" Lana screams as black claims me.

LANA

J can't stop the tears falling down my face. Astarot lies in a huddled pile on the floor, not moving. I can't even see if he's breathing. This isn't the way it's supposed to be. He has to be okay.

Nausea grips my stomach, doubling me over. It passes in a shuddering wave leaving me feeling even emptier. It's hard to breathe. I have to know he's okay.

Rising, I look over at the pirate who stares at me but doesn't react. Okay, deep breath, walk forward. The floor vibrates hard, with the occasional jump as if they're driving over any obstacle that gets in their way. Putting a hand on the ceiling to steady myself, I make a tentative step towards Astarot, keeping an eye on the pirate.

One step then another but he doesn't stop me. When I reach Astarot, I kneel beside him, taking my eyes off the pirate for the first time. Though I'm not looking at him I'm paying attention with my other senses. I won't let him take me by surprise again. Astarot taught me better. I shouldn't have let my guard down the first time.

My hand shakes as I reach for Astarot. Clenching it into a

fist I try to steady it before I touch his brow. He's cool, but that's not unusual. He's always cool to the touch, no matter how hot it is. Sliding my hand along his cheek I bring it to rest on his neck, hoping that he has an artery where I can feel his pulse in somewhere close to the place it would be if he were human.

Stopping and closing my eyes I feel for it, but nothing. No, no, no, he's okay. He has to be. This isn't how it ends for us. I slide my hand forward and wait, feeling for the pulse that has to be there. Nothing, damn it. Biting my lip hard enough to taste blood I move my hand along his neck again and feel. There! It's slow, steady, but, but a pulse. He's alive.

Relief floods through me causing my tears to flow even more. My head is pounding, my mouth is dry, and crying isn't helping anything. Knowing he's alive though, that's enough. It means there's hope. The pirate grunts, stomping his foot on the floor. Glancing over my shoulder, he motions me away from Astarot.

Reluctantly I crawl backwards, trailing my fingers across him until my outstretched arm won't reach him any longer. Back on my side of the space I lean against the wall and let the vibrations of the transport lull me into a fitful sleep.

I WAKE, THANKFUL TO LEAVE BEHIND THE NIGHTMARES THAT chase me through sleep. Every part of my body aches, deep down to the bones. Stretching doesn't touch it. My head pounds, my throat is dry, and my stomach feels like a ball of acid boiling over. Random waves of nausea grip me then pass. Something is wrong, way wrong, and I don't know what, but I feel like shit.

The guard, I assume it's the same one as they all look alike, stares at me then grunts or maybe he says something.

Shame burns for an instant as I consider how racist my thoughts are but what do I know of space pirates? They all look orange, leathery, and have the same hair style.

Pulling my feet under me, I rise, but the nausea hits hard then the room is spinning and I drop back onto my butt. Okay, that was a bad idea. Shaking my head to clear it does no good. Hell with it. I crawl over to Astarot. His eyelids flutter when I touch his cheek then open.

"Astarot," I plead.

"Lana?" he asks, his voice cracking.

Moving closer, I want to kiss him, but a sharp grunt accented by the slam of a boot on the floor stops me in my tracks. Looking over my shoulder, the pirate grunts several times in a row then raises his gun which makes his intentions clear. I pull back, unwilling to risk it.

"Are you okay?" I ask.

He closes his eyes, his nostrils flare, then he opens his eyes and nods.

"I'll be fine," he answers. "Are you okay?"

I nod, my throat clenching tight and refusing to allow words out. Tears fall but I wipe them away. I can't cry, not now. Sniffling, I wipe my nose on my sleeve then nod, biting my lip.

"Yes, I'm fine."

"I'll get us out of here," he whispers. "Just need time."

"I know," I say, and I do.

I don't know how or why, but I know he'll save us. My faith in him is absolute. My belief that no matter what comes, we'll handle it is complete. The transport jerks hard and I'm tossed to the side. Looking around, the guard looks as surprised as we are.

"What's happening?" I ask.

The vibration stops, then it feels like we drop to the ground. The door towards the front slides open with a screech of metal on metal and two more pirates walk into the space. One points at me, growling and grunting. The guard answers, puffing his chest out and stepping into him. They argue then the third one puts a hand on each of their chests and pushes them apart.

The two stop talking and step back. The third one, who seems bigger than the other two, walks towards me. My heart pounds in my chest so loud it's a drum in my ears. I'm light-headed and my vision wavers as my breath comes faster and faster until I realize I'm hyperventilating.

The larger pirate towers over me, staring down, beady eyes looking me over like a piece of meat. There's no hint of a soul in those dead eyes. His huge hand comes at me and grabs me by my throat, lifting me to my feet. The chains holding Astarot clank as he struggles against them but the new pirate ignores him.

Setting me on my feet, he let's go of my throat but his hand runs down my chest pushing my torn shirt open and exposing my breasts. He stares as if he's never seen a pair of tits before in his life then grunts, growls, and looks over his shoulder. My chest and face burn hot as I take the chance to cover myself.

The Zzlo walks away, ignoring me. He slams his hand against the wall next to where I've been sitting. Something whirs and then a crack forms in the wall outlined by a blinding, red-white light. The whirring sound grows louder as the wall lowers. The bright, red suns of Tajss stream through, blinding me. My eyes water as I blink trying to adjust to the new, bright light.

Shapes move out into the light through my bleary vision, more heard than seen. Wiping the tears from my eyes I blink until at last I can see. The side is a gangplank, the same one they led us in. The three pirates have gone outside leaving no one to watch me.

Astarot nods. Pursing my lips I take a tentative step towards the door. The red suns make the rolling sand look like it's dotted with sparkling diamonds. Stopping in the opening, I let my eyes adjust once more until my vision clears at last. A massive black shadow dominates the horizon.

It looks almost like... but it can't be. We've traveled to far for...

Our crashed ship? Shaking my head, I walk down the ramp feeling numb. The shape is wrong. Something isn't right, it's not the wreck we landed in. That means, no, it can't be...

Nearby, screams tear me away from the shadow forcing my attention much closer to home. Two people are running with the pirates in close pursuit. One pirate whirls something over his head, it's a flashing blur that flies when he releases it. It takes one of the fleeing figures in the legs, knocking them to the ground.

The other stops to help the fallen one, and it's over. The pirates surround them, bind them with practiced, brutal efficiency, then drag the bound forms towards the transport. Cold chills run across my skin adding to the overall crap feeling of everything hurting. As I turn to walk back in to Astarot, a wave of nausea clamps my stomach and I drop to my knees, crying out.

"Lana!" Astarot yells.

Doubled over in pain, I clench my arms across my stomach until the cramps pass.

"I'm fine," I lie, panting through the pain.

"What's wrong?"

"I don't know," I tell him, gritting my teeth as I push my way back to my feet.

Moving to my place along the wall, I take my seat and hang my head, hoping to go unnoticed. The metal ramp clangs under their boots. The shouts and screams become clearer now. They drag the new captives in despite their struggles.

They captives kick and try to fight their way free. Afraid of attention, I stare at my feet, watching out of my peripheral vision as they're dragged in. My heart leaps into my throat and I gasp. Humans. They captured two human women.

"LET ME GO!" a curvy red head yells.

The pirate is dragging her by her bound hands. She's kicking, rolling side to side but to no avail. The pirate tosses her like she's nothing. She flies and lands on the far side of me with a yelp and a whoof of exhaled air. It takes all my will to not react. Stay calm, don't attract attention.

"I will kick your ever loving ass!" another female voice from outside the transport sounds.

I hear her long before they get her up the ramp. The sounds of struggle outside the open door echo through the metal box we're in. The pounding in my chest, a pulsing desire to help, to do something engulfs me. No, we can't win, not yet. Glancing at Astarot in his chains I know I'm not strong enough to take out three pirates.

Outside the pirates grunt and then raise their voices. One of them makes a sound that might be pain or surprise. Go girl, whoever you are, get away! I cheer her on but fear keeps me frozen in place.

"Damn you space bastards!"

The sickening thud of flesh on flesh is followed by a yelp of pain then silence. Clomping of boots on steel then the other two pirates walk in carrying a figure between them, one with the shoulders the other holding the legs. Stopping just inside the box they swing her between them like a sack of potatoes then send her flying to the back of the transport.

She slams hard against the rear wall without a sound, making it obvious she's unconscious. Booted feet appear in my limited vision as I continue staring at the floor between my feet. A loud slap of leather on metal then the open door screeches and grinds shut.

The three pirates move to the front of the transport, talk for a minute, then two of them go through the sliding door leaving us alone with our guard. Silence engulfs the room, broken only by the soft sobbing of the curvy red-head girl. Swallowing hard, I try to force my heart back down into my chest.

Humans. Another piece of the ship. Survivors. Other survivors. We're not alone.

The implications are staggering. My head hurts too much to think it through and the aching of my muscles is just growing worse. I'm hot and dry. So dry. Too dry.

"Shit," I exhale, realizing what's wrong with me.

Astarot opens his eyes locking with mine.

"What?" he asks.

The guard stomps his foot, making a loud echo that hurts my ears, and then grunts. Astarot's lips tighten and his hand balls into a fist. The muscles of his arms flex then relax. If he was free that guard would be in trouble.

"Epis," I mouth the word.

His brow furrows, confusion on his face, then his eyes widen and his mouth opens. I nod to show him I see he got it.

I'm not just suffering dehydration. I'm going into withdrawal. The negative side of taking epis. It's addictive and, in theory at least, withdrawal is a killer.

ASTAROT

*N*ew humans. I don't recognize them, where do they come from?

My bonds cut into my flesh, tearing, biting through my skin and leaving me chafed. Shifting, I strain until I can see the new additions. One of them is a pretty, curvy girl with a bright red mane. Her face and eyes are pink and swollen with falling moisture.

The other is dark-skinned, a warm color that reminds me of the eyes of a bivo. She's hurt, lying in a ball not moving, but I see her sides rise and fall so she's not dead. Her hair is short and curly, pretty, different. She fought the slavers the hardest. I heard her screaming though I didn't know what her words were.

Where did these women come from? They aren't from Drakonov, that much I know, so where?

The transport hums, vibrates, then it feels like we rise before it jerks into motion. We're off again, to where I don't know. Testing the bonds I stretch and pull, searching for any weakness. They used a rough rope to bind my tail and wings which seems to get looser the more I work it. Chains bind my hands and feet but if I can free my tail, I can be deadly enough.

Lana pulls my attention. The guard watches as she moves over and sits down next to the red-maned female. They talk in their common tongue. Rapid fire words going back and forth. I should learn it but the sounds are difficult. Shidan did it, so it's not impossible, but I've never needed it before.

The new girl glances at me and I can only call her look one of fear. Why she seems just as afraid of me as the pirates I don't understand, but humans are strange. They talk for several minutes. I want to know who they are, what they are doing, where they are from, but I can't do anything about that. Instead I focus on what I can do something about. Closing my eyes I inhale as deep as I can then exhale it all, collapsing my chest to its limits. This loosens the bindings on my wings and tail a little. Shifting my tail, the rope adjusts giving me the smallest bit more leeway.

"There are others!" Lana says, cutting into my breathing exercises.

"I see that," I say, opening my eyes.

"No, not just these two, others!"

Lana's voice lilts up and her smile is bigger than I've ever seen. The girl next to her looks between the two of us then says something. Lana answers her then they engage in another long conversation. I wait, patient, certain she will return to my own questions in time. It gives me time to work on the bonds. When the talking stops, I open my eyes again and arch an eye.

"You look too logical when you do that," Lana says.

"What do you mean?"

"Like Spock, you're all cold and logical," she says.

"Who is Spock? Do I know this person?"

Lana shakes her head. "No, forget it. Bad analogy, I never

liked those shows, anyway. I will not sit through hours of them just so you can get a joke."

"Okay," I say. "So, the others?"

"This is Olivia," Lana says, pointing at the female next to her. "There's another section of the generation ship out there!"

She turns and points behind her through the wall.

"Another?" I ask, thinking about this.

"Yes!" she exclaims.

"And more survivors,," I say.

"Yes, she says there are a lot of them," Lana says, speaking rapid fire once more to Olivia. "You're the first Zmaj they've seen. She's afraid you might eat her."

Lana laughs but I frown. Eat her? Humans can be so strange.

"How are they surviving?" I ask.

Lana shrugs then talks with Olivia more.

"They have supplies from the ship," she says.

"I see. Is that one okay?" I ask.

Olivia sees me look at the unconscious female then her eyes widen and she's talking fast and loud. Loud enough the guard growls, stomping his foot on the floor and cutting off all conversation. After a few minutes Lana talks to her, speaking softly to avoid the pirate's ire.

"What is going on?" I ask, waiting as long as I can.

"She's scared of you," Lana says.

"Why?"

"You're different," Lana answers, as if that says it all.

"So is she," I observe. "No wings, no scales, no tail, very different."

Lana laughs before she continues speaking to Olivia.

"They're surviving on their own," Lana says, surprise in her voice. "No Zmaj, no epis, but they're surviving."

I understand her surprise, mostly, but right now the only

thing that matters is getting free. Four pirates, when they stopped there were still only four. If I plan it right, I can handle four pirates if they don't have those weapons. Get free, take out the one here with us. It needs to be quiet, fast, so I can be in position when they come through that door. The door is a block, only one of them can come in at a time. As soon as it opens, take out the first two then it's one on one. Don't let them use their weapons.

"Can you believe this?" Lana asks.

"What?" I ask.

I haven't been following their conversation. It sounds like gibberish there are so many hard sounds in the human tongue. It's not rough or guttural like the Zzlo but still difficult for me.

"No Zmaj," she says. "No epis."

"Why is this surprising?" I ask, confused.

"I don't now, it's just, I thought we were the only ones," Lana says.

She rises and goes to the other girl. Kneeling, Lana touches her face then pushes until she's lying on her back. In a flurry of action the girl jerks, rising fast, and hits Lana in the chest knocking her back. The girl is yelling something as Lana crawls away holding her hands up and talking fast. I lean into my bonds trying to move between Lana and her attacker. I move forward the few inches the chains allow.

The dark girl looks up at me then screams. It's a wordless, warbling sound, her eyes wide, then follows it with a stream of fast hard sounds as she backs away. The guard stomps forward, Lana is shouting, Olivia shouts, and I hiss at the girl who attacked Lana. Confusion rules the small space.

The rope holding my tail slips further then blood rushes back with a tingling, painful celebration of its sudden freedom. Holding it close to my body, gritting my teeth against the anguish of it, I remain still. The Zzlo stomps past me, standing between the dark girl and I, holding a hand out towards each of us.

One chance, this is it. I take it.

14

LANA

*O*livia screams, the pirate is yelling and stomping the floor with his boots, Astarot is leaning into his chains then everything turns to chaos.

The pirate reaches for his gun but just then he's falling. Astarot hisses, almost a roar. His tail! It's free!

A sickening crack as the pirate's head hits the floor reverberates around the room.

"Kill that son of a bitch!" Delilah, as Olivia called her, curses, scooting towards the downed pirate.

She raises her bound legs and kicks the pirate in the head, then like a madwoman she keeps doing it. Astarot strains against his bonds, the muscles of his arms and chest bulging, the edges of his scales tinting to a deep shade of red.

Staring, I'm lost. I should act, but do what?

Knife. On the guard's belt is my knife which he took while capturing us. Diving forward I grab it from his belt. The familiar weight of it in my hand gives me an anchor. Something solid, sane in the midst of the confusion. What do I do with it?

Astarot is hissing louder, his muscles straining so hard

I'm sure he'll burst a vein. Flipping the knife over in my hand I step behind him and slice through the rope binding his wings. As the rope drops they spread wide, reaching side to side of the cargo space, and I stumble back.

He doubles his fists up and slams them into the guard on the ground. The guard grunts, lifts his head, Delilah kicks him again at the same time. The guard's head bounces off the steel floor and he lies still.

Silence.

The four of us stare at each other in sudden silence. It's strange, scary, like the world is a new and different place. My heart beats a slow, steady rhythm despite all the excitement. Feeling calm, I walk over to the guard, kneel, then sift through the pockets attached to his clothes.

I toss aside the extra bits and pieces until I find a ring of keys. There are a dozen of them and I have to try all but the last one before I find one that clicks in Astarot's shackles.

He grabs me before the falling cuffs hit the floor and sweeps me into a kiss, wrapping his arms and wings around the two of us. Delilah gasps.

"Lana!" Olivia yelps, fear in her voice.

They're in the distance, somewhere over there, I'm here with Astarot. Relief cleanses my body, pushing aside the ache, the pain and the parched feelings. The emotional release is so strong I can forget how bad I feel for at least this time. His lips on mine, his strong, muscled arms holding me tight, makes the world right.

"You've got to be kidding me," Delilah exhales.

Astarot lets me go, his wings folding back into place. My cheeks burn hot with sudden embarrassment.

"What is the matter?" Astarot asks.

"Nothing," I answer.

"What are they saying?" he asks, looking at the other two.

"It's nothing," I say again. "What do we do now?"

Astarot rolls his shoulders. "Finish this," he hisses. "Free them."

"Are you two..." Olivia says, then trails off, not finishing her thought but I know what she was about to ask.

All the old feelings jump out. I'm ashamed, not of Astarot as much as just who I am. A vagrant. Unwanted, extra, I don't belong. It's ridiculous but I can't help what I'm feeling. I don't meet either of their eyes as I unlock their bonds.

"Yo, whatever your name is," Delilah says.

"Her name's Lana," Olivia adds.

"Sure, got it, Lana. What the hell is going on? What is he? Why are we with," she kicks the pirate, "these?"

Simple question, complicated answer.

"Let's focus on getting free first, then we'll share more stories," I say, pushing aside all my regrets, fears and worries.

"Yeah, good plan," Delilah agrees.

The two women keep what distance they can between themselves and Astarot. Astarot ignores them.

"What's the plan?" I ask him.

"I'll stand to one side of the door, make a noise, when they come through, I'll take them out," he says.

"Are you sure that will work?" I ask.

He shrugs in response.

Doubt niggles at my thoughts but I don't have a better plan. Astarot moves over to the door.

"What is he doing?" Olivia asks.

"There are at least two more of them, we'll lure them back here, then take them out."

"I will give them more than that," Delilah says, her voice hard.

Astarot looks at us then motions with his hands. The girls don't argue as I translate and get us all moved out of the line of sight. Astarot looks around, frowns, then goes to the downed pirate. He drags him towards the door and arranges him. Looking at it, I can see his plan. It looks like the guard collapsed and he's right in front of the door, creating an extra barrier to them entering the room.

He looks everything over once again then reaches out and bangs on the door. Holding my breath I wait but nothing happens. Gasping, I take a deep breath then hold it again as Astarot hits the door even harder. The vibration and sense of moving slows then the transport jerks, coming to a stop. Exchanging quick glances with the other two women I tighten my grip on my knife. Delilah has a length of chain with a heavy metal cuff swinging from her hands, ready to use it. Olivia looks fearful, crouching down to one side to stay out of the way.

The metal door screeches, sticks, then jerks open. Astarot explodes in a flurry of motion. My eyes won't follow the action it's happening so fast. One moment we're all standing there then he's moving and there are grunts, groans, and Astarot is standing in the doorway with three pirates out on the floor.

"Damn!" Delilah exclaims.

Pride fills my heart and I'm beaming at my man. My man. What the hell am I thinking? No, it's true. All considerations aside, the way I feel with him. He's mine and damn I'm a lucky woman.

"Hurry," Astarot says, motioning. "Grab their gear, supplies. We need to get out of here."

"We should take the transport," I say.

"Do you know how to operate it?" he asks.

"Let me look," I say.

"Are you talking with, him, it, whatever that is?" Delilah asks.

"That is Astarot," I reply. "Yes, I am talking with *him*. You think I kiss random guys I can't even talk to?"

Her chocolate skin darkens a little, showing she has the decency to blush at least. I smile to ease the sting.

"Sorry, he's just, I mean..." she motions with her hands at Astarot.

"He's a dragon, sort of," Olivia fills in. "An alien, an honest-to-goodness alien dragon-man."

"Yeah," I say. "Trust me you get used to it. He's also our best hope of survival."

Sliding past Astarot, I move up to the front of the transport. The controls are strange and foreign. One look and I know I have no idea how to operate this thing.

"Let me look, too," Delilah says, sliding into the small front space.

There's only room for the two of us, Astarot stands outside in the crossover hallway.

"Can you drive it?" I ask.

Delilah sits down, touches things, pushes buttons, does stuff I have no clue about then shakes her head.

"I think it's broken," she says.

"What the hell happened? It was just running," I say.

"No clue but I'm sure this should start it up and it doesn't," she says pointing at a panel. "This flashing here, might be some kind of fail safe."

She leans in closer to the flashing screen.

"A fail safe for what?"

"Shit," she exhales. "We have to go. Now."

"What? Why?"

"It's not a fail safe, its a locater signal and a radar. There's another thing approaching fast."

Cold chills fill my stomach and I follow her back into the transport.

"Astarot, we have to go, there are others coming," I tell him.

We grab what gear we can carry and then head out into

the desert. As soon as the door opens the heat washes over and my knees grow weak. Just for a moment everything turns gray and the room spins. Astarot's arms are around me, holding me up.

"Lana!" he exclaims, catching before I fall.

"I'm fine," I say, struggling to remain upright.

It passes as fast as it hit, leaving me feeling more tired than I was before. Pushing off of Astarot I meet the open stares of the women.

"Are you okay?" Olivia asks.

"Yeah, sorry, it's just…" What do I tell her? I'm going into withdrawal from an alien plant? "The heat."

"I get that!" she says, chuckling. "This place is hotter than hell."

"It looks like Vulcan," Delilah adds, standing on the ramp going down. "Barren and hotter than a firecracker."

"Yeah," I say. "Well, you're in the Star Trek camp, I see."

Astarot keeps an arm around my waist, leading me down the ramp. I don't want to show it but I'm grateful. I'm not sure I can stand on my own right now. My muscles are spasming at random intervals. It's not too much of a problem but it's making standing upright harder than it should be.

"We need to move," Astarot says. "Can you get them to move faster?"

"Sure," I say, then translate the same over to them.

We walk across the desert headed for who knows what. It's hard work made harder because of how bad I'm feeling. I need epis. We weren't supposed to be gone this long. I don't even know how long we've been out or how far from home we are. The transport moved us fast and far.

"Home is this way," Delilah says, as we top a tall dune.

I say as much to Astarot. He stares out across the desert then turns a slow circle. When he finishes his turn he frowns.

"What?" I ask.

"We are far from our home," he says.

"Kind of figured that," I reply.

"What is he saying? How can you understand those hisses?" Delilah asks.

"There's a machine back home, in Drakonov," I say.

"Drakonov?" Olivia asks, her eyes widening. "You mean, like a town? You call it that?"

"Well, it's a city," I say.

"A city? Do you have running water? Toilets? Oh do I miss a good toilet the most," Olivia exclaims.

"No, we don't," I say. "It's an abandoned city, well mostly, or it was. Ah, it's complicated."

"Are there more of," Delilah nods at Astarot.

"Yes, some," I say. "We're working together to survive."

"I think he's hot," Olivia says, her fair skin turning a deep shade of pink.

"You're just dehydrated and lonely," Delilah says.

"Sure, but still, look at those muscles," Olivia says, somehow blushing harder then looking away.

"We need to get to our home," Delilah says, bringing the conversation back on point. "We need supplies."

"True, how are you all surviving the heat? It's been a long time since the crash. You haven't seen other Zmaj?"

"Z-ma-shhh?" Delilah asks, sounding out the word.

"Ju," I say. "Zmaj."

"Ah," she says, trying it again and getting it closer. "No, we haven't seen anyone like him. Those bastards who got us are the only aliens we've run into."

"I told Patrick the others weren't just missing, now we know. Odds are they were captured by those orange assholes too," Olivia says.

"Pirates," I add, trying to be helpful.

"Pirates?" Delilah asks.

"Yeah, they're the ones who attacked the ship and caused us to wreck," I say.

"Well we need to get back," Delilah says, brusque and all business. "The camp needs to know and I don't want to be out here in the desert without supplies. I'm already feeling dry."

"What do you think?" I ask Astarot, telling him they want to go to their camp.

"Do they have epis?" he asks.

"I don't think they know what it is," I reply.

"You need epis," he answers.

"Yeah, but what else can we do?"

Frowning, he nods, then we all walk in the direction that Delilah pointed.

"So you're all surviving on your own, what about food? How do you deal with the heat?" I ask, a million questions dancing in my head.

"We have supplies from the ship, but we've also gotten some crops to grow, so we're good on food," Olivia says.

"You look terrible," Delilah says. "How long have you been out in the desert?"

"A few days, I think," I answer her.

"Just a few days?" Olivia asks, surprise in her voice.

"Yeah, why?" I ask, defensive.

"You look a lot worse than a few days," she observes.

"Yeah well, that's the epis withdrawal."

"Epis withdrawal?" they ask as one.

I explain epis to them while we struggle our way across the sand. It takes time because I keep running out of breath. The sand seems to get softer and harder to walk through. Astarot has to help me most of the time. I can't find the strength to do it on my own. Everything hurts too much.

"So," Delilah says. "You and the dragon-man, huh?"

The suns are setting at last, bringing the welcome relief of nightfall.

"Uh, yeah?" I'm too tired to talk.

"Are you two, you know, doing it?" she asks.

I stop, blushing hard. "What of it?"

"Well, are you, how did you figure out you're, you know, compatible?" Olivia asks, jumping into the conversation.

"Yeah, what's he like down there?" Delilah asks, grinning from ear to ear.

"Look, I'm not go-"

The surrounding ground explodes. Sand flies into the air, blinding me and getting into my mouth. Choking, waving at the air, something pokes into my ribs.

"Lana!" Astarot yells, grabbing me and pushing me behind him.

We're surrounded. Three shadowy figures close in, sharp spears poking at us, forcing us back into each other.

15

ASTAROT

Surrounded. Anger rises, bijass closing in. The three figures drive us back with their spears. Turning, I try to keep them all in my sight but it's impossible. How did the pirates find us?

"Astarot," Lana says, her voice low, quavering with fear.

"It's fine," I say, holding my hands up.

The three surrounding us are wearing large, flowing cloaks with hoods that cast their faces in shadow. They don't look like Zzlo. So who are they?

"Shut up," one of them says in Zmaj.

"What?" Lana and I exclaim as one.

A bigger, bulkier one reaches up and pulls the hood off his head. He's a Zmaj with blue and yellow edged tan scales. He narrows his eyes, glaring at me.

"Shut. Up," he says, accenting each word. "No speaking."

"You're Zmaj!" Lana says.

He turns towards her. Red edges my vision, my muscles quake as I struggle to suppress and control my rage. He steps in close to my treasure, too close. Lana doesn't back down, straightening she stares up at him, defiant. He hisses, and she holds her ground. My hearts pound hard, filling my ears with the pulsing of blood. He leans over her trying to dominate.

I leap, slamming into his side and knock him to the ground. Air whoofs out of him as we hit the sand rolling, locked in a struggle for dominance. A roar rips from my throat as the rolling stops and I'm on top. Pounding my fists into his face he raises his arms to protect himself. His tail slams into the back of my head knocking me forward.

"Astarot!" Lana is screaming.

I can't stop, if I do they'll win. I have to save her, she's my treasure. He can't touch her.

Pressure on my arms, pulling backwards. I'm drug off of him by the other two. Struggling against them I strive to break free but their grip is too strong, I can't. The one I was beating climbs to his feet. Wiping blood from his mouth, he rolls his head causing his neck to crack loudly. He walks towards me, slow, his hands balling into fists.

"That was a mistake," he hisses, then his fist slams into my face.

My head jerks to one side, my teeth slam together, and something pops in my neck. Looking up at him, I grin, blood dripping down my chin.

"That the best you got?"

He growls and raises his arm back.

"Ragnar," one of the males holding me says, and he stops.

"What?"

"We should take them to the elders," the other one says. "You know the edicts."

"Burn the edicts," Ragnar says.

"I'll burn you, that's my female," I hiss, straining forward and forcing the two holding me to tighten their grip.

"Only if you can keep her," Ragnar growls, leaning in until we're face to face.

"We could kill him," the other one says.

"No," Ragnar says. "Edicts are edicts. They are what hold us together."

"Edicts make us one," the two holding me intone, as if it is some kind of chant or mantra.

I stop struggling and they let me go. I have no target for my rage. The three others move to stand side by side. The other two lower their hoods and I see they're also Zmaj. None of this makes sense. Zmaj don't live and work together. What is this mantra they're chanting?

"Astarot?" Lana asks

The other two human females are talking to Lana, wanting to know what is happening.

"It's ok," I tell her before asking the foreign Zmaj, "Who are you?"

The big one, Ragnar, shakes his head.

"We're the Tribe," he answers. "What are you doing here?"

"These are mine," I say, pointing at the women. "Zzlo captured us and I fought them, made our way to freedom, but now we're far from home."

"How far can you be? These are Sky Folk, they come from over there," he points off behind us.

"You've seen them before?" I ask, shock hitting me like cold water.

"Of course," he answers.

Lana moves beside me placing her hand on my arm. Ragnar watches, his eyes drifting to her exposed skin showing through her torn shirt. Anger flashes white hot, clouding my thoughts, my hands ball into fists. I struggle to not attack.

"That's a different part of the ship," Lana says, her soft, beautiful voice cutting through my rage.

She speaks to the other two women while the three new males watch us.

"Come on," Ragnar says.

"Where?" I ask.

"To the Tribe," Ragnar says, as if that answers all my questions. "The Elders will want to see you."

"We're not going anywhere," I growl.

"I didn't say you had a choice," Ragnar says, stepping closer.

He puffs his chest out and I step into him, matching. My tail shifts side to side, he flutters his wings, and I spread mine wide.

"These are my females," I say, voice low and soft.

"Only if you can keep them," he says. "Edicts are edicts. Edicts bring us together."

"I don't know what 'edicts' you're operating on," I say. "You want to take my females I'll destroy you."

He snorts and the edges of his scales tint red with anger. His mouth tightens into a hard line as a smile spreads on my face.

"Ragnar, stop," one other says.

"Astarot," Lana says and I dart a glance in her direction.

Her and the other females are in a huddle watching.

"What?" I ask.

"We should go with them. We're a long way from home."

Ragnar and I glare at each other for a moment longer before I step back, conceding the space. She's right and this entire display is the bijass, pushing towards conflict and not resolution. I can't give into it.

"Right," I agree. "Lead the way."

Ragnar takes a moment longer than I do to let his rage go. He shakes himself all over then turns and walks off into the desert. Our group falls in behind him. Lana walks at my side, the other two females drop in behind. One of the other Zmaj falls into step on my other side.

"He's not all bad," he says.

"Yeah?"

"I'm Bashir," he says.

"Astarot," I say.

"That's Melchior," Bashir says, pointing out the unnamed Zmaj.

Melchior is moving ahead and off to the side. He moves fast, staying low to the ground with his head moving left to right in quick succession as he scouts ahead.

"Where are we heading?" I ask.

"The Tribe," he replies.

"What is it?" I ask.

Bashir gives me an odd look like I might be crazy. Shaking his head he picks up his pace and walks away. If nothing else Lana is right. I don't know where we are in relation to home or how to get us back there. I'm also curious what this 'Tribe' is. Seeing three Zmaj working as a team is strange enough but their weird mantra and the things they say are worse.

Elders? Tribe? Sky People?

The new Zmaj look primitive. They don't have lochabers, which is a traditional weapon. The spears they're carrying have rough metal tips that look crudely forged. They're wearing leathers that look rough. The other Zmaj, back in Drakonov, all have their lochabers and good clothes. We're not wearing home-made leathers, yet. The three of them make hand signals back and forth as they walk. I'm sure they're communicating but it means nothing to me.

"Are we in trouble?" Lana asks, whispering.

"We're fine," I lie.

"You're a terrible liar," she says. "Your scales turn green when you try it."

Frowning I hold my hand up to see what she is seeing.

"There's no green," I observe.

"I know, but now I know you're lying," she smiles.

"Okay, I don't know," I say.

"Yeah, isn't this strange? I thought Zmaj couldn't be around each other? Aren't we the exception back home?"

"I thought so too," I say. "We struggle with it there. Somehow these three have figured out a way to avoid the bijass."

"Maybe they can help us get home?"

"Be careful what we say," I tell her.

"What do you mean?"

"They may not be friends."

"Oh," she says, her mouth snapping shut.

We walk in silence. Lana stumbles and I help her then the other females who are moving slower too. Moisture is pouring down their faces, soaking their clothes. I have to help all of them as the new males keep marching, ignoring them.

A mountain range has been coming closer for a while now and we're climbing the outermost hills of it. They're following a path up the side. I'm not sure if it's natural or created but it turns back and forth allowing only two Zmaj abreast. The girls walk three abreast but they're small.

Ragnar and Bashir lead the way while Melchior has fallen back and brings up the rear. Climbing and climbing until I can see out across the empty desert for a long ways. There's a shadow in the distance, rising towards the sky, something massive sits there.

"That's the ship, I think," Lana says, following my gaze.

"It's bigger," I say.

"Yeah," she agrees.

There's something in her voice I can't identify.

We turn another time then we're passing into a breach of the rocks. The walls squeeze in tight and Ragnar has to turn sideways to get through. I squeeze through but it's tight. When we emerge I stop and Lana runs into my back.

"What?" she asks. "Astarot? You okay?"

I can't answer her. I can't believe what I'm seeing. Looking down into a small valley with dark cave openings dotting the walls on either side, there are Zmaj. Over two handfuls, maybe even more. Several of them stop and stare at us. Ragnar's wings spread out from under his cloak, he raises his spear over his head and hisses loudly.

16

LANA

I can't see past him. Pushing does no good, he's too big and solid.

"Astarot!" I yell this time, wanting his attention.

He still doesn't move.

"What's happening?" Olivia asks from behind.

"I don't know," I say.

Giving up on making him move, I squeeze past, scraping my back on the wall.

When I turn and look I know why he's standing there. This isn't supposed to be. I'm staring down into a valley with cave openings dotting the walls. Zmaj men move around the valley floor, in and out of the cave openings, talking to each other and working. There must be a dozen of them, maybe more. The sight of it takes my breath away.

"I thought you couldn't stay with each other?" I ask, awe in my voice.

"We can't," he says. "This is… impossible."

"Come on," Bashir says, motioning us forward.

Ragnar stares, shaking his head. His wings flutter and his tail shifts side to side in an agitated movement.

"How?" Astarot asks the hunters.

"The Commander can explain, quit wasting time," Ragnar hisses, turning his back on Astarot.

Astarot tenses, his hands balling into fists. His anger is palpable, so I put a hand on his arm. He turns his head towards me, his jaw tight, his lips pursed, anger burning in his eyes.

"It's okay," I assure him.

He blinks several times then his hands unclench. Ragnar has gone a distance ahead of us so we follow him down into the valley. The two new women whisper between themselves. Today has been one long series of firsts. Tajss was devastated in a massive war years and years ago, the handful of survivors found that they were regressing to a more primal state, one they call bijass. It made it impossible for them to be around each other without fighting, so they separated, each going their own way to wait out the death of their race.

That's the story, that's what we know. So how are all these Zmaj living together? A clanging sound of metal on metal echoes off the stone walls of the narrow valley. Inside an alcove in the wall a large Zmaj is pounding out metal at a forge. He doesn't look up as we pass, intent on the white hot metal he is shaping. Another we pass is working large pieces of leather, preparing it in the sun's light.

Most of the Zmaj pause in what they're doing and look up as we pass. No one says anything. Ragnar and the other two lead us to the back of the valley where it ends in a box. As we approach a dark rectangle that can't be a natural occurrence in the rock, the biggest Zmaj I've ever seen steps out into the sunlight. He's so tall and broad he has to duck and turn sideways to fit out the opening.

Crossing his arms over his massive chest that looks broad enough for me to lie down on, he frowns down at Ragnar.

Ragnar glares up even though he himself has to be seven feet tall. The new Zmaj must be almost eight feet tall. His scales have a subtle red tint to the tan. He doesn't have the bright colorations at the edges that most Zmaj have either. His brow is heavy, his jawline strong and sharp.

"Get out of the way Drosdan," Ragnar hisses.

Drosdan's wings flutter, spreading part way out and casting a shadow across Ragnar. His thick tail drags on the ground making a shifting sound.

"No," he says, not moving. "What is this?"

"It's for the Commander, not you," Ragnar answers.

"No one sees the Commander," Drosdan says.

Ragnar's tail goes still and I can see his shoulders tense. His head tilts to one side.

"You wouldn't," he hisses.

"I could," Drosdan says, making a sound that is a cross between a snort and a laugh.

"Edicts," Ragnar hisses.

Something passes over Drosdan's face. Anger, rage, regret, submission, it's fast and makes me even more curious. What are these edicts? How do they keep these Zmaj living and working together? It's more than obvious that Drosdan wants to beat Ragnar and just on size alone he probably would. He doesn't, and that leaves me wondering.

"Edicts bring us together," Drosdan says, reluctance in his voice, then he steps to one side.

Ragnar steps through the opening into the darkness and the rest of us follow. Drosdan glares at each of us as we pass. Astarot meets his gaze, not breaking eye contact until he is through the door, straining his neck to keep contact as long as he can.

The air is cooler inside. As my eyes adjust to the dim light we're led down a straight, smooth tunnel cut into the rock.

The floor inclines down until it levels off then we enter a room lit by candles. The flickering light casts dancing shadows across the red stone walls. Three chairs sit against the wall opposite of us, the center one occupied by a male Zmaj with a hood pulled over his head and a staff in his hand.

Ragnar walks over and stops a few feet in front of the seated Zmaj. Ragnar bows at his waist, his wings spreading part way out from under his cloak. He remains bent over in that position waiting.

"Edicts are edicts," a soft, hissing voice says from inside the seated man's hood.

"Edicts bring us together," Ragnar responds, then stands up and steps to one side.

Delilah, Olivia, Astarot and I exchange confused looks, none of us sure what we're supposed to do next. The Zmaj before us leans forward, his staff rapping on the stone floor. Taking the hood in his hands he slides it off his head.

It's difficult to tell a Zmaj's age. Their longevity keeps their bodies young much longer than a normal human life-span, but this one seems older. Something about his eyes, I think. We stare at each other without speaking, I'm waiting for a clue what to do next.

"Welcome," the seated man says at last.

"Thank you," Astarot replies, taking a step forward.

Two more Zmaj enter the room from an open doorway to our left. These two are definitely old. Their hair is thin and gray, their scales are dull, lacking the normal shine of a Zmaj. Their shoulders and backs are bent and they both walk with heavy sticks, leaning on them for support. They go to the other two chairs without a glance at us and take their seats.

"I am Visidion, Commander of the Tribe," the first Zmaj says. "You've already met Drosdon outside, my Second."

"I am Astarot," he says, bowing at his waist. "This is my mate, Lana, and my females."

The hair on back of my neck bristles when he calls me his mate but there's a pleasing warmth in my belly. Ragnar grunts but the two to either side of Visidion lean in and whisper in his ear, talking low and quick.

"Good," Visidion says. "These are the Elders of the Tribe. Kalessin, Founder and my Father, and Falkosh."

He motions to his left then right as he introduces the two others.

"Be welcome," Kalessin says, his voice is a leathery whisper like a soft touch on my skin that gives me goosebumps.

There's a heavy wisdom in his voice you can feel when he speaks.

"If you wish to stay with the Tribe, you must agree to and follow the edicts," Visidion continues. "If you will not, or cannot, we will give you supplies and send you on your way."

"What are the edicts?" I interject.

The four males besides Astarot all turn and look at me in obvious surprise. My cheeks burn hot as a sudden urge to crawl under a rock takes over. There is no pulling back the words now I've put them out there. I hear Ragnar hiss to my right. The three seated males look at each other then back.

"You speak our tongue?" Visidion asks.

Feeling lost and desperate I look at Astarot for guidance. He purses his lips and his clenches his jaw. Shit, what have I done? Running a hand over my face I pull myself together.

"Yes," I say, my stomach rock hard, and my heart racing.

The two Elders lean in close to Visidion and whisper behind their hands. I can't make out what they're saying but there's no doubt it's about me and my ability to speak Zmaj. Astarot takes a step closer so our arms are touching while he remains half a step in front of me. I swallow hard, trying to force moisture back into my mouth.

The Elders sit back, staring at me, while the Commander, Visidion, seems lost in thought. When at long last he sighs and rises fear knots my stomach. I don't know if we're about to go to war or what. There are a lot of Zmaj here and there's no way that Astarot can stand against them all alone. I'm under no illusions that I'd be of any help.

"We need you," Visidion says.

"You can't have her," Astarot says, his voice tight.

Visidion looks Astarot up and down in quiet contemplation. Ragnar makes a sound, his wings and tail shifting, but doesn't come closer.

"Yes," Visidion says. "We have much to discuss."

"We appreciate your hospitality," Astarot says. "But we need to get back to our home."

"This could be your home," Visidion says. "What have you out there to return to?"

Astarot's mouth snaps shut. I can see he doesn't want to say too much and I'm not sure I blame him. How much do we trust these people we just met?

"Ah," Visidion continues. "I see, you need understanding."

"Yes," Astarot says, taking the offered way out.

"Come," Visidion says, walking past Astarot.

"What is going on?" Olivia asks in Common, her voice quavering.

"Do we need to run for it?" Delilah asks.

"It's fine," I tell them. "I think."

"How are you defining fine?" Delilah asks.

Good question. How am I defining it? Smiling at the two girls I shrug.

"We're not out in the desert with no supplies?" I offer.

All of this is being made harder by how bad I feel. The

muscles in my arms and legs tremble, my mouth is dry, but the headache is below a dull roar, so that's nice at least.

"Okay, points for that," Delilah says and Olivia nods her agreement.

"Look, right now I don't know what's happening. I'm struggling to keep up but I'll tell you when I know something."

Olivia bites her chapped lips. Her skin has an almost gray tint to it and her eyes look dull and lifeless. Delilah doesn't look much better. They need epis.

"Fine," Olivia agrees.

Astarot follows Visidion outside the shelter. The bright suns are high enough overhead to stream down into the valley, burning my eyes even worse. Rapid blinking helps my eyes to adjust, but doesn't relieve how dry they are.

"This is the Tribe," Visidion says as we gather in a semi-circle.

To make life easier on the other humans I translate for them as he speaks. Visidion watches me do this, his head tilting to one side. A tingling sweeps up my neck and across my face. Why is he watching me with such interest? Astarot follows his gaze then looks back.

"What?" I ask, unable to take the scrutiny without doing or saying something.

"It is nothing," he says. "Allow me to continue, all will come clear. The Tribe is what we call ourselves. We are the product of my Father Kalessin's vision. After the Great War he gathered those he could. Knowing our fate and that the bijass was rising, he developed the edicts."

"Yes, what are these edicts?" Astarot interrupts.

Visidion smiles in response. "They bind us, one to another. Simple in concept, powerful in application," he says.

"Beautiful words that have no meaning, what are they?" Astarot asks, baring his teeth in frustration.

"One, I am myself. Two, together we are stronger. Three, survival of the group matters."

"That's it?" I ask, surprised when he stops talking.

Watching Astarot who seems lost in thought, maybe they mean more to a Zmaj? They look too simple to have any great effect like saving the entire Zmaj race or forcing them to work together. Visidion flashes a smile at me but his attention is on Astarot.

"Simple? Yes," Visidion says, like he read my mind. "They are a tool, they focus the mind. The true control comes from within us, our inner strength only needs a focus to exert itself."

"I see," Astarot says, nodding.

"Come, see what we have accomplished," Visidion says, resuming his walk. "We have craftsman for leather, stone, and a blacksmith. Our hunters you have met, led by Ragnar, they provide us with food."

Walking down the length of the valley Visidion points out the different craftsman to us. At the blacksmith's alcove there is a smaller Zmaj, the smallest one I've ever seen, though still bigger than a human man. As we approach, he grabs something from a shelf and walks away. The blacksmith, a huge Zmaj even by their standards with large, bulging arms, drops his hammer and grabs the smaller Zmaj by the back of the neck. Spinning him around he backhands the smaller Zmaj who drops the item. Only then does the big man release him and he falls to the ground.

The smaller Zmaj stays on his knees as if he's groveling before the blacksmith. He picks up the item he dropped and holds it over his head offering it to the blacksmith who takes it, puts it back on the shelf, then takes back up his hammer and resumes working like nothing happened.

The entire scene makes my breath catch in my chest and my heart pound with regret and pain for the smaller Zmaj.

The casualness of the cruelty is unacceptable. Olivia gasps and Delilah curses under her breath but none of us move to intervene. Visidion walks on by as if nothing happened.

"Is that how you treat each other?" I ask.

Visidion stops and turns around. He glances at the blacksmith who's ignoring us. The smaller Zmaj has gotten to his feet and wandered off into one of the openings that lead into the cliffs. When Visidion looks at me I see a hardness in his eyes and the set of his features.

"It is a struggle, every day, to control the primal. The edicts bind us, guide us, but strength is strength. Strength is how the tribe survives. The weak, those who cannot contribute..." he shrugs. "Each member of the tribe brings something to the group. Those who do not, they are on their own."

Those who cannot contribute... I know all to well that mentality. My life on board the ship crashes into my brain. That part of me wants to protect the outcast because he is like me, unwanted. Never allowed to contribute. I could have, I was able, just not permitted. Maybe all that Zmaj needs is a chance to find his calling.

"Hey, they're leaving us behind," Olivia says, putting a hand on my shoulder.

Startled, I jump into motion, lengthening my stride to catch up to the group. There's a small path that winds up to a second level of door openings carved into the rock face of the valley wall. The group is about half-way up it when we catch up. Visidion stops outside of one, turning back to us.

"This is what you can help us with, the future of our race," he says to me.

Future of their race? "So what is it you need?" I ask, cutting to the chase.

We walk into the cool tunnel that leads down for a ways. Flickering light ahead draws us forward. The floor doesn't slant down like the other room we were in, this one is level, leading deep into the rock. As we move, the soft sound of voices drifts closer, echoing off the rock making it impossible to distinguish any words. There's a softness to the voices though. Children? Do they have Zmaj children here? The voices are too soft for males.

"Oh," Astarot exclaims, as he steps to one side of the tunnel letting me pass.

"What?" I ask, but then all thoughts flee.

Three human women sit in a circle around a table talking with each other while eating. They've turned to the opening and fall silent on our entrance.

"Lana?" an older woman with gray hair at the temples of her shoulder-length auburn hair and crows feet at corners of her eyes says.

"Mom?" I gasp, a cold feeling racing out from my core as my stomach flutters like a million butterflies dance inside of it.

She rises from the table, the chair she was sitting in falls over and clatters to the floor. Her mouth is open as her eyes widen and tears fall. Raising her arms towards me they tremble while her mouth moves. She shakes her head side to side as she moves around the table.

"Oh Lana!" she says and bursting into speed we run into each other's arms.

I cling to her with desperation and unbelief. It can't be. I can't believe it's her. This is some kind of horrible delusion and I'm sure that at any moment it will be ripped away. Her arms hold me tight, just like she always did. Her scent fills my nostrils. She smells like mom, that mix of antibacterial soaps with a slight hint of violets, her favorite flower. I'm crying but no tears stain my cheeks, dehydration and withdrawal from epis have taken those. My chest shakes with heavy sobs but I can't let her go. I want to pull her into me.

"You're alive," I sob into her shoulder.

"You know her Bailey? Astrid? Penelope?" Olivia asks.

The room explodes into rapid fire conversation but none of it has anything to do with me. My mom is alive and holding me tight. Fear it will all be a dream keeps me from letting her go.

"I've missed you so much," I tell her, my face buried in her hair.

"Oh sweet baby," she says. "I thought I'd lost you."

I don't know how long we stand holding each other, neither of us able or willing to loosen our embrace. Her chest heaves, her body shudders, as she sheds her tears. She grips my shoulders and pushes me back to arm's length. Her stormy gray eyes alight with her deep intellect as she evaluates every detail.

"You're sick," she says, and it's not a question.

"I'm fine," I lie, my smile faltering. Her insight was never something I could hide from.

With tight, pursed lips she nods then shakes her head and pulls me into her again.

"Later," she whispers. "Right now I'm just glad to hold you again. I love you, my sweet baby."

I'd forgotten how good it felt to be in her arms. Wrapped in the security, feeling her unconditional love.

"I love you, too," I say.

Taking a deep breath and wiping at my face, I step back to look around the room. Olivia and Delilah are talking rapid-fire with the other women. They're talking over each other in their excitement. Visidion and Astarot are behind me, watching us. Astarot focuses on me, shifting from foot to foot. His tail moves back and forth so fast it looks like he's trying to take flight. Mom is looking over my shoulder at him then she looks at me with an arched eyebrow.

"Uh, yeah," I say unable to meet her gaze. "Mom, this is Astarot."

"He's one of them," she says.

"Yeah," I say. "He's a Zmaj."

"A what?" she asks.

"And she speaks their language too, also I think she's boning that one!" Delilah says from behind my mother.

My toes curl as a wave of nausea grips my stomach. I glare at Delilah but she's taking a hundred miles an hour ignoring me. My mom clears her throat but I can't meet her gaze.

"Is there something you want to tell me Lana?" Mom asks.

Shrugging, looking at my feet and struggling to control the nausea, I shake my head then shrug.

"Astarot," I say in Zmaj. "This is my adopted mother."

I can't look at either of them. God, I'm so embarrassed I could die. Astarot steps closer, towering over my mother and me too. He smiles, holding his arm out to her. My mom takes his hand.

"You're a big one," she says and I translate that to him for her.

"Please tell your mother she is a beautiful sparkle on the sands and it is my great honor to meet her. I will gladly share water with her."

I look at him feeling incredulous.

"What?" I stutter and he repeats himself. "Where did that come from?"

"She is your mother, I want to honor her," he says, tilting his head and furrowing his brow. "Do my words not translate to your tongue?"

"They translate, just…" I trail off, my thoughts whirling in a maddening circle. "Okay, sure."

I translate his words for her and her face lights up.

"Well," she says, grinning. "I like this one."

Disbelief and the absurdity of the entire situation cuts through my embarrassment and at last I can just relax.

"Of course you do," I reply.

"You hush," she says, then we're both laughing.

"How are you here?" I ask.

She looks over my shoulder, anger and fear vying on her face while looking at Visidion.

"They captured us," she says.

"Captured?" I ask. I whirl on Visidion. "You captured them?"

"We rescued them," he responds.

It's easy to see this is all a matter of perspective but that won't make it any easier to sort out. It's obvious what they need me for now. I'm the only one that can talk with both groups here. It's also obvious I've got my work cut out for me.

One of the new women talking with Olivia and Delilah falls to the floor. My mom rushes to her side while the other girls cry out in surprise. Mom kneels down touching her face and neck.

"Get the water!" Mom barks and one girl hands her a clay cup.

Mom holds the girl's head up and pours water into her mouth, forcing it past her lips. None of the women look healthy. They all show signs of extreme dehydration. I thought Olivia and Delilah were in bad shape but they are pictures of health compared to the women here. That makes sense since they were just captured by the pirates. Who knows how long my mom and the others have been here.

"They need epis," I tell Astarot. "Soon or they won't survive."

"I know," he says.

"What do you mean they need epis?" Visidion asks.

"Epis, they won't survive without it. Do you have any?" I ask.

"No," he says. "It's too dangerous. We don't harvest epis any longer. That is the old ways."

"The old ways need to make a comeback or these women will die."

Visidion frowns, shaking his head.

"This will take much thought," he says.

"You don't have time for thought, why are they here? Why did you capture them?"

"We did not capture, we rescued them," he counters.

"Rescued, captured, either way I'm assuming your plan wasn't to bring them here to die."

"No!" he says, his eyes widening and his nostrils flaring with anger. "They are treasures, they are our future."

"Good," I say, stepping up to him and pointing a finger into his chest. "Then you best get your thinking cap on because if we're going to save them, we need epis and we need it fast."

ASTAROT

*T*here's a flash in Visidion's eyes that makes my scales itch. Putting my hand on Lana's arm, I push it down.

"They need epis, now," she says, her teeth gritting. "That's my Mom!"

"I know, let me help," I tell her.

Her glare cuts me, stabbing into my heart but at last she nods, giving me her trust.

"Fine," she says, making a chopping motion with her hand. "He better help."

Turning back to Visidion he's staring at Lana.

"Can we walk?" I ask.

"Of course," he says, motioning towards the door for me to lead the way.

Watching over my shoulder I see he watches Lana until we're outside and she's blocked from view. Only then does he turn his attention back.

"She's... different," he observes.

"Yes," I say. "She's human."

He nods, thoughtful and quiet.

"Tell me more of the Tribe," I say, hoping to calm any upsets.

"What would you know?" he asks.

"How? I remember the gatherings after the devastation," I say. "Our race was at its end, we all agreed. The bijass was too strong, so we separated to live out our days alone."

"True," he says. "That is how I remember it was well."

"Then how," I motion around us at the workers.

More Zmaj are moving in and out of what must be their homes. They are all busy, working on something. As we walk down the valley two Zmaj in front of us stare each other down. I can feel the tension, my bijass rises to it, a dark, throbbing need that threatens my control. The bigger of the two, hisses, his wings spread, his hand balls into a fist and I know he's about to swing.

"Edicts are edicts," the smaller Zmaj says.

The bigger one stops, nods, "Edicts bring us together," he intones stepping aside and letting the smaller one pass.

"It's… incredible."

"Maybe," Visidion says. "My father deserves the credit. He created the edicts. They don't always work. The Zmaj has to be strong of will. Lacking that the edicts are nothing. They only give focus."

"I see," I say. "How long has this community been here?"

"Long enough for my father to grow old and me to grow wiser," he says. "How do we mark the passage of time?"

We walk as we talk. The ringing of metal on metal grows louder as we approach the blacksmith's work area. Watching him work as we approach I can see his craftsmanship is impressive if not up to the standards of old. Before the devastation there were machines that did his work, but his work by hand is effective if not pretty.

"Greetings," I say, raising my voice over the ringing of his hammer.

He looks up from what he's working on, grunts, then resumes hammering.

"My brother, Padraig, isn't one for words," Visidion says.

"Can you make a lochaber?" I ask.

Padraig lets his hammer stop on the anvil, resting it beside the piece he's working on. When he looks up he's glaring, his jaw tight, his eyes narrowed.

"Are you being cute?" he asks, his voice a low hiss. "What's wrong with the one on your back?"

"Nothing," I say, struggling to not meet his hostility with my own.

Strangely enough the edicts of the Tribe come to mind.

"Does it look like I have the tools for fine work like a lochaber?" he motions around himself. "We're lucky I can make spears for the hunters."

"Can you make a spear for me then?" I ask.

"Can I or will I?" Padraig asks.

"Ah, pay no mind to old Padraig!" the Zmaj that works next to him says.

This Zmaj has built an awning that sticks out from the alcove he works on and is the one I saw earlier working on a hide. Different hides and leathers lie on the tables around him making his trade obvious.

"I meant no offense," I say.

"He's just mad that his work never comes out as pretty as mine," the new Zmaj says. "I'm Arawn."

"Astarot," I say, reaching out and grasping his arm at the elbow which he does in return.

"Your work looks like majmun dung," Padraig says. "And I don't work for free, stranger."

"I could trade," I offer. "What do you need?"

"Nothing you have," he growls.

"Padraig could you be any less of a zemlja on a bad day?" Arawn says, shaking his head.

Arawn has an easiness to his nature that makes you want to like him.

"Shut up before I shut you up," Padraig says, taking back up his hammer.

"You came with the new females, didn't you?" Arawn asks.

"Yes," I say, my eyes narrowing.

"Well there you go," he says.

"There I go what?"

"Padraig here needs a female," Arawn says. "Help him out there and you'd be doing us all a service."

Padraig slams his hammer down on the anvil with great force. In one step he closes the distance between Arawn and himself, grabbing the other Zmaj by the front of his shirt and lifting him off the ground. Arawn laughs, waggling a finger in his face.

"Now, now, Padraig," Arawn says. "Edicts are edicts."

Padraig shakes Arawn, tightening his grip.

"Brother," Visidion warns.

"Edicts bring us together," Padraig says, setting Arawn down then turning his back.

Arawn laughs and turns his back on Padraig, returning to his work.

"What trade?" I ask Padraig.

"Nothing for you," he says, slamming the hammer down on the anvil.

The ringing echoes off the valley walls causing my ears to ring in time. The bijass rises, demanding I show him my strength, that he is not better than me. He will listen when I speak. My muscles quiver, thrumming with the adrenaline pumping into them.

"Trade," I repeat.

Padraig's hammering stops. He meets my glare with his own. I struggle to remain in control, my hands clench tight enough I can feel my nails digging in.

"A ration of water," he says, dropping his eyes.

My bijass roars triumph, making a grab for control but I'm able to stop it. I take a deep, cleansing breath then I look at Visidion.

"What is a ration?" I ask.

"A system of trade," he explains. "We work together, each producing for the tribe but trade makes it fair. Water is the most valuable, so it is a standard trade. A ration is one day's worth."

"Agreed," I say, understanding.

I stick my arm out towards him waiting for him to accept the deal. He stares at my arm, the heavy hammer in one hand. Turning his head, he spits, sets down the hammer then steps over and takes my forearm, sealing our deal.

Padraig goes to his work and Visidion walks away so I follow. I can't help drawing comparisons between the Tribe and Drakonov. The human influence on Drakonov and us Zmaj becomes obvious.

Why? Why the differences?

Padraig and Arawn display it clearly for me. Strength still rules, a nod to the bijass. That is what our primal instincts demand, domination while bowing to those that have proven stronger than you and even then reluctantly. The edicts, their mantra, may keep them out of their bijass but their society bends to it still.

In Drakonov we aren't having this problem. Why? The humans are the difference. All the Zmaj males in Drakonov have mates or in my case I'm working on it. The other males aren't locked in as deep. The females are the key.

"What do you think?" Visidion asks.

"It is nice," I say, careful to not say too much.

Do I tell them about Drakonov? I don't think so, not yet.

"Carefully chosen words," Visidion says.

We're walking back along the length of the valley. The best answer I have for him is to ignore his comment.

"The humans need epis," I say, changing the subject.

"It is too dangerous, there must be another way," he says.

"How are you surviving without it?" I ask.

Zmaj don't have to take it often, not like the humans, but we need some at least every couple of years.

"Epis is the root of chaos, we have cleansed ourselves of it," he says.

"Cleansed?" I ask.

"Yes, epis caused the downfall. Epis made us slaves. We are free now."

"Free from what?" I ask. "There's no future, our race is dying."

"Then we will die with dignity, but the females bring us hope," he says, stopping and turning towards me.

Narrowing my eyes, I study his face trying to understand what he's thinking.

"That makes no sense," I say.

They can't know we're compatible with the humans. No one in Drakonov would have known if Calista had not borne Ladon's child and that was a surprise to everyone. Does Visidion know the females can bear our children? If so, how?

Visidion smiles then taps his staff against the sandy stone of the ground. Three times he raps and as with so many things here there is an air of ritual, though I don't understand it. There is nothing I can remember from before like that but then I lost a lot of my memories to the bijass.

"Kalessin is a Seer," he says, rapping three times more. "He foresaw the war, he tried to warn the Council, but they ignored his pleas. He foresaw what would come and prepared. Through his vision we have what we have. When the great fire appeared in the sky, he saw then that our future had arrived. He knew females would come and fill our need."

"He 'saw' this?" I ask, incredulous.

"Yes," Visidion says, his face straight and serious.

He's not joking. I'm not sure what to make of this. Visions and telling the future aren't something Zmaj do, do they? The gray fog of time that conceals my memory swirls as I try to dig through it but nothing comes.

"Well," I say, at a loss for words. "What are your plans for the females then?"

"Your female, Lana, will help us. We will learn to communicate. They will each find willing and happy mates among the Tribe. Visidion has told us."

He speaks with such conviction it's clear there is no arguing with him. These are just facts waiting to happen.

"No one will force themselves on the human females?" I ask.

Visidion frowns, shaking his head. "Of course not, we are Zmaj," he says.

I nod my agreement. If they're not intending to force the females, then I have no argument.

"Good," I say.

"They will become treasures. Already they call to their mates though they may not yet know it. They will, it's only a matter of time. Look how Lana came to us in our time of need."

I can't argue his logic even if it is unrealistic. I need to talk with Lana, somewhere quiet. I don't intend to stay here forever and before her mother I was sure she didn't either. That changes things.

No matter, we have to get back to Drakonov, they need us. The Zzlo are growing bolder that much is obvious. As well there is an entire new camp of humans and the Tribe to talk with them about. The future of Tajss is changing.

"The suns are setting, I should get Lana and rest," I say.

"You'll have shelter," he says. He motions with his staff

and the smaller Zmaj that I saw groveling before Padraig earlier runs up from somewhere. "Samil, show our new friend to his quarters."

"Yes, Commander," the small Zmaj says, his head bowed the entire time.

He leads me to an opening in the rock and inside I find a small sleeping area. There are unlit candles, furs for a bed, and a small storage shelf.

"Thank you," I say, turning towards him in time to see him flinch as I move.

"Yes," he says, bowing his way out of the room.

Civilized? Perhaps, but they are still slaves to the bijass. I light candles then go to find Lana and bring her home for the night.

18

LANA

"*I* can't believe she's alive," I say, following Astarot into the cave-room they've given us for the night.

It's small but functional and gives us some privacy. Candles push back the darkness. Astarot grabs one of our packs and pulls out food for us, I sit down on the pallet of furs and leather. My head is pounding and I feel like I can't get enough air. A cold sweat forms on my arms although the room is hot with dry, still air.

Astarot kneels, offering me some of our dried guster meat. Chewing it eases the pain in my body. Guster use the epis caves as their hatching grounds and the babies feed on epis, infusing their meat with some of its properties. It's trace amounts but enough to fool my body into thinking it might get its 'fix'. Leaning my back against the cool, stone wall I chew and contemplate the day.

Mom is alive. It's a miracle. Something I hadn't dared hope or think of. She's here and there are other survivors on the planet. This changes everything!

"I'm glad," Astarot says, sitting down next to me.

"It's so... strange," I observe. "I'd just not thought about it, you know? I'd accepted the loss, that's the way it was."

Astarot shrugs, chewing his food. He places an arm across my shoulders, so I rest my head on his chest. The relief that comes with the guster meat is growing less. If I don't get epis soon, I'll be in trouble.

"None of this is expected," he says.

"Did you talk with the Commander more? Will he help us to get epis?"

"I'm not sure," he says. "These males are... strange. I don't understand them or their ways."

"What do you mean? Is it all that different from what Tajss was like before the war?"

"Very much, yes," he says.

"How?"

Astarot chews thoughtfully and silently for several minutes.

"They don't use epis," he says. "Or so he claims."

"They don't?"

"No," he says. "Visidion says they're cleansed of it. Epis was the lifeblood of Tajss. It was our product, we traded epis across the galaxy. Everyone took it. Epis was life, it infused every part of our society."

"Yeah?"

He shakes his head hunching forward. "I don't know," he says. "It's different."

"Well, one way or another the other women won't make it without epis. The section of ship they crashed in had a hospital so they have supplies, but that will run out. Our bodies won't hold up to this heat without epis."

"Then we'll get epis," he says, straightening. "One way, or another."

I touch the cool scales of his finely muscled arm, flooded with warmth and there's a fluttering in my chest. Leaning closer I strain for his lips and he obliges, turning and moving in until our lips meet.

He pulls me closer, my body melds to his as a fire inside roars to life. Trembling as I kiss his sweet lips, his strong hands move down my back, drawing me in. Lifting he turns us both, lying me down on the furs. I'm engulfed in him, running my hands across his delightfully chiseled chest. The muscles flex as he moves, my skin tingles anticipating his touch.

I pierce his lips with my tongue, seeking his. Our mouths move as one, his cock pushes hard into my core, trying to drive past the thin fabric separating us from our desires. My fingers trail across his folded wings. His weight presses me into the floor, solid and real.

The edges of his scales have red and green tints that pulsate with his desire. His chest warms under my touch, taking my warmth in as I will take him.

The coolness of his touch slides along my skin, making its way under my shirt as he pulls it up and over my head. Pleasure so intense it's painful explodes as my nipples harden to diamond tips. A low growl escapes his throat when he looks down, then his hot mouth is on me and I cry out my pleasure, biting down and trying to keep quiet.

Can the others hear us?

The thought flees before the circling of his tongue. Let them. I don't care, he feels too good, I need him too much.

The pressure of his restrained cock pressing between my thighs is making my legs quiver. I can't wait any longer. I need him in me and now. Trailing fingers across his hard stomach, I loosen his pants, pushing them down. His cock bounces free, the hard ridges along the top like a series of waves on an ocean, leaned back and ready for my pleasure.

I slide my pants off, awkward while we continue kissing and touching. My lips burn, desire is all consuming. The head of his cock is at my opening, I grasp his ass and pull but he doesn't come forward, holding himself over me.

"Astarot," I pant.

His beautiful lavender eyes stare into mine, he kisses, soft, fast kisses across my cheek, up to my lips, down the other side. Holding himself up with one arm, his free hand strokes my face, down my neck. His lips meet mine with butterfly kisses, repeating as his hand grasps my breast. Taking my nipple between his thumb and forefinger he pinches and I cry out, a wordless sound of pleasure.

Jerking in response it forces his cock into my pussy. The first ridge stops further entry. My body adjusts, growing wetter, then he lowers himself into me, one ridge at a time as my pussy adjusts to his girth. No matter how many times we do this each time is like the first. His girth, the ridges on the top of his cock, are the limits of what my body can handle.

It expands me, exposes nerve endings never stimulated. I'm breathing in ragged gasps, my heart pounds at a hard gallop, butterflies fill my stomach. I'm alive. He pushes in until the ridge at the base of his cock powers through my soft folds and finds my clitoris.

As that hard protrusion makes contact, my body explodes into a thousand stars shooting through the night. A gasp escapes, wordless sound that doesn't express the sensations rocking my body. That contact on my most sensitive nub is pleasure beyond belief or experience.

He grinds his hips into me, moving deep inside and against my clit. Fire burns through every nerve followed by freezing cold. Sensations too many, too fast, its electric running across all my skin. I'm burning with it. Consumed in the fires of our passion. He pulls back leaving an emptiness behind he fills with a single thrust forward.

"More!" I cry out and he obliges.

He takes me. Pounding hard into my pussy, filling me

over and over, the exotic scent of him fills my nostrils as his cock fills my pussy. The weight of his thrust satisfies on a deep primal level. He grunts, panting hard with exertion and desire.

His grunts become my name and that is enough to push me over the edge. I fall into the molten sensations of all consuming desire as I'm taken. I become one with him as he thrusts in and unloads his seed. Holding himself deep inside, his throbbing cock pulses in my pussy, we kiss.

Collapsing back onto the mat my legs feel like jelly. My heart is pounding like a thousand horses in my chest. I concentrate on breathing, slowing my heart as I return to awareness. When he pulls out it's a loss, leaving an emptiness behind. His second cock is hard and ready but I'm not. Somehow, no words are necessary for him to know this. He rolls off of me, lying down, and I scoot in close' resting my head on his chest.

His heart has a double rhythm beat. It's calming and relaxing as we lie, entangled with each other, soft touches. I'm enamored with him. No one has ever made me feel the way he does but how do I balance that with what I want? I can't be 'his' and be a hunter too.

I've seen how the other Zmaj are. They can't stand to be apart from their mates. If I commit to him he'd never be okay with me leading a hunting party of my own. I'd never stand on my own. The other humans would never look and see they need me. I'm valuable, I keep them alive.

Thoughts circle my mind as I trace my fingers along the muscles of his chest, feeling the cool, smoothness of his scales. I can't, even though I want to, I can't be his the way he wants me to. I have to prove myself and find my place in the world. My choice of mate can't define who I am.

It would be nice... I think as the gray blanket of sleep pulls me into its embrace.

19

ASTAROT

"We don't need it, why do they?" Ragnar asks, the same question he's been posing all morning.

"Can you not see they're different?" I ask, frustration tightening my throat.

The urge to punch him in his smirking mouth is almost too much. The bijass circles the edge of my awareness, ready to pounce, prodding at my control. Ragnar isn't making it easy. He's arrogant, condescending, and overall a jerk. He's also the main thing in my way of getting what I want.

"I see," he says. "The females we saved were doing well and they've been here for a long time without epis."

"Are they doing fine now?" I yell.

He smiles as he steps back, rolling his shoulders.

"We'll find a way," he says, shrugging, but his eyes watch my shoulders, ready for me to attack.

If I didn't know better, I'd think he's trying to provoke me. Maybe he is. Is this part of the culture of the Tribe? They have a might makes right attitude. What's his game?

"How long do you think you have?"

"Kalessin will guide us," he says, like it's a matter-of-fact.

He believes it, too. I've never seen anything like it. Zmaj don't act this way. His faith in the Seer irks me. I don't know how to deal with it. They're all this way too. How can they have such strong belief one male's vision?

I've never even heard of a Seer before. I may not remember everything from before the Devastation but I'm sure I'd remember a Seer. There's never been such a thing on Tajss before. There was no belief, I remember. We worked, that's what we did. We harvested epis, shipped epis, epis was life. Everyone on Tajss worked to produce epis in some capacity.

"How can you be so sure?" I ask, shaking my head.

"Because he has and he will, he has the sight."

His words shut the door. There is no arguing with his blind belief. Even if I could, how do I? Kalessin brought the Tribe together, through his 'vision' or just insight I don't know. There's no arguing with the results. Before the humans crashed, I and all the other Zmaj now in Drakonov were living alone and waiting to die. Surviving because that's what we did, having no contact with any others.

"They need epis," I say, throwing my hands up. "Their bodies cannot take the heat of Tajss. There is no other way!"

"We'll see," he says, laughing and shrugging.

The bijass leaps forward, his smug face fills my vision. My fist swings faster than thought. He leans back, ready for it, blocking the blow.

"Edicts are edicts," he hisses.

Edicts. I don't care. Rage burns white hot. I'll wipe that smug smile off his face with my fists.

Edicts. It cuts through my rage. *Edicts are edicts. Edicts bring us together.*

"I apologize," I say, lowering my fist.

Ragnar nods his acceptance. "Maybe it's just your female," he says.

"What?" I hiss, the rage rising again.

"Perhaps you're not man enough for her," he observes. "I might challenge you for her."

Struggling to maintain control I have to force words past the tightness of my throat.

"She would never..." I trail off, unable to force words out.

"Oh?" he says, glancing over his shoulder at me. "Females like strength. If I bested you, she'd see I was the better mate."

I'm shaking I'm so angry. Red edges my vision as I turn away from him. Don't look at his face. It only makes it worse the way he smiles. He's goading me. I won't give in to his taunting.

Lana needs epis. I need his help to get it.

"Yes!" I hear Lana's voice.

"Ah, there she is," Ragnar says. "What beauty!"

We're walking past the part of the valley where the craftsmen are working. She's standing next to the leather worker, Arawn. They're both engrossed in something on the table before them. The leather worker laughs, pointing, then says something but I can't catch the words.

My stomach turns sour. Lana reaches in front of the leather worker, touching something on the table. He reaches forward, his hand resting on hers, moving it. My jaw hurts as the sickness in my stomach turns to a burning pain. My breath comes faster, my nails dig into the palms of my hands. She moves, then her hip is against him. His arms reaches around behind her.

"Enough," I growl.

"Hmm?" Ragnar asks. "Oh well, maybe I've already lost that one. She seems quite taken with Arawn."

"ARGH!" I scream, pushing Ragnar out of my way and storming towards the table.

Lana looks up, smiles, then her eyes widen.

"Astarot, no!" she yells, holding her hands up in front of her.

Arawn looks up, his eyes widen as his mouth drops. His wings open and he takes a step backwards. Grabbing the table between us I toss it to one side. Bits of leather and tools fly and there's a loud clatter as objects hit the ground. Swinging as I close, my fist takes him under the jaw.

His head snaps back, clacking shut. He stumbles, falling backwards, coming up against the stone of the valley wall. I'm on him. Pounding, his head slams back and forth. He grunts and swings his tail but I block, then strike in a blow I know will numb the muscles making it useless. Strong hands grab my arms. Yelling. Sounds of struggle. Breaking free I hit him again, this time punching into his chest.

He slides down the stone as I'm drug away. Hands are on me everywhere, grabbing my arms, my legs, someone has my tail. I fight them all. None of them will have her. She is mine! My treasure!

Red fills my vision, laying over all the sights. I scream my rage.

Lana's face. She's shaking her head. Her mouth moves, but I can't understand what she's saying. Tears, she calls the moisture from her eyes tears. I don't understand. Why the tears? I'm saving her.

"Astarot," she says, putting a hand on my chest.

The coolness of her touch is calming. Chill spreads from where her hand rests. My hearts slow, my breathing returns to normal, the red rage recedes. I stop fighting the ones holding me. Soon they ease their grip and I'm put back on my feet.

Two Zmaj kneel next to Arawn, helping him to his feet.

He stands bent in half, hands on his knees. When he looks up, wiping the blood from his mouth and panting, he shakes his head then straightens. He's hurt but doing his best to hide it.

We stare at each other then he looks over at Lana and back. He makes a slicing motion with his hand between us. The hands holding me let go.

"Outsiders," they mutter, walking away.

"Edicts," someone else hisses.

I'm left standing alone. Lana looks horrified. Arawn is walking over to the table I threw, groaning as he bends to pick it up. I go to help him.

"Let it go," he hisses as soon as I touch it.

"I'm sorry, I want to-"

"Go," he says, making that same cutting motion with his hand. "I don't need your help."

Straightening, I look at Lana. She shakes her head then turns away. A stabbing pain drives into my chest and I can't breathe.

I lost control and now I've lost everything.

20

LANA

*H*is eyes bore into my back but I refuse to turn around. I can't believe he did that. I'm mortified. Avoiding looking at Astarot, I help Arawn in picking things up and putting them back on the table. It's not long before I hear Astarot's footsteps as he walks away.

"I'm sorry," I say, setting a stack of cured leathers down on the table next to Arawn. "I don't know what came over him."

"It's fine," he says, rubbing his jaw.

A drop of blood trickles from the corner of his mouth. Taking a cloth from the table I dab at it and see him wince at my touch.

"No, it's not. I've never seen him like that before."

"It's the bijass," Arawn shrugs. "We all struggle with it."

"That doesn't make it acceptable!" I answer, my face flushing as I slam my hand down on the table. "He shouldn't have done that."

Arawn places a hand on my fist, soft and gentle. When I look up at him he smiles.

"You don't understand," he says. "The bijass, it's always there, waiting."

"No, I don't understand. What is it? Why?"

Muscles quiver as tears fall. My throat and mouth are dry, my head is pounding. I feel like shit, like I've been through a ringer and then tossed aside in a pile. Every muscle aches, each breath takes an effort because expanding my chest hurts. I don't need this crap. Astarot acting that way, it's just too much.

"It's instinct," he says, putting down a handful of tools before turning to gather more.

His tools and leathers are all over the place. Next to us, the steady ringing of Padraig's hammer pounds in time with the pain in my head. I can't tell if it's helping or making the pain worse. Padraig hasn't stopped working. I saw him look over when Astarot was beating on Arawn, I thought he might help, but he shrugged and resumed his work. Until Astarot had Arawn up against the wall, then he intervened.

"Instinct," I snort. "What does that mean? I've got instincts, I don't act on them all the time. I'm not an animal."

Arawn gives me a look I can't read. He smiles, shakes his head, then rises with a load of leathers and carries them to the table.

"Zmaj are different," he says. "Apparently."

"You think?" I ask, motioning between the two of us and laughing for the first time since this happened.

Arawn smiles. He has a nice smile, its bright, lighting up the space. I like Arawn, he's funny.

"Well, I mean more in a…" he shrugs and laughs. "I don't know human males. Are they not… protective? Do they not treasure their women?"

"No, not like Zmaj do, it's different."

"I see," he nods, thinking. "When a Zmaj mates, it's for life. She is his treasure, his everything. He will do anything for her. She becomes the center of his universe."

When he speaks his eyes take on a far away look, like he's

looking into a distance much farther than the wall of the valley. There's a wistfulness to his voice and I know what that means.

"You've picked one," I observe.

"Hmm? Oh, no, ridiculous. A mating has to be mutual," he says, brushing aside my observation.

"Uh-huh," I let him off the hook, but I know.

It's obvious he's chosen one of the human women, I wonder which one?

"The bijass is a reversion to our most primal instincts," he continues, changing the subject back.

"Has it always been there?" I ask.

"No," he says. "Well, yes, but no. Before the Wars, it was different. I think parts of it were there but our entire society accommodated it, it was less somehow. There weren't the problems we saw afterwards. Something in the war, the loss, triggered us."

"That must have been terrible," I say.

He smiles, a sadness falling over his usually happy face. His mouth moves like he will speak but nothing comes out. He moves away gathering the last of the things scattered in Astarot's rampage.

"So your shoe idea, I think this new design will work," he says.

"I think so," I say, letting him change the subject, again.

"Your initial pattern is good. Using the hardened bivo leather and these reinforcing bones here, should let you move across the sand almost as good as a Zmaj."

"Great," I say.

Moving in beside him we set to work creating the first of my sand shoes. It's fun work, seeing my vision come to life and the time passes by quickly. The shadows are encroaching before I know it and my belly is growling. Being engrossed in the project I can push back how crappy I feel.

Kneeling, I fasten the shoes to my feet while Arawn watches, grinning. Leather strips serve as laces which I pull tight. When I stand I'm off-balance. Arawn reaches out, catches my arm and steadies me.

"Okay," I say, letting go of his arm.

"Ready to try these out?"

"Damn straight," I reply.

The floor of the valley is mostly stone and my feet are heavier with the new shoes. It makes moving different. My center of gravity isn't the same. It doesn't take me long to figure it out and I'm making my way out of the valley. Arawn walks along with me, close enough to help if I need it.

Once we're outside the valley, I stop and look out over the open desert. A hot breeze shifts the sands across the dunes. It looks like massive snakes crawling along sand. The setting suns cast an almost purple light across the red, whites, and golds of the planet surface giving everything a surreal feel.

Arawn and I grin at each other then I step onto the loose sand. I put my weight down slow, tentative, prepared to sink but hoping I won't. The shoe takes my weight, nothing cracks, so far so good. Shifting my full weight to my right foot, I bring my left forward and place it.

"They work!" I exclaim, jumping up and turning.

I land perfectly and don't sink.

"I see that!" Arawn agrees, laughing.

I take off running across the sand. Arawn paces along beside me. The shoes work just like I hoped they would. They're small enough to not inhibit my ability to move too much but big enough to distribute my weight and keep me on top of the sand.

I have to show Astarot!

As soon as I think of him my guts clench tight. I'm still mad about what he did. There's no excuse for his behavior but I miss him already. I want to share this moment with him, not with Arawn. Though I couldn't have done it without Arawn too. The joy is gone out of the moment so I stop running.

"We should head back," I say.

"Yeah, the suns are low, sismis will be out soon."

We walk back in silence until we're back inside the safety of the valley.

"Thanks for all your help," I say.

"It was fun," he says. "Nice breaks from my normal work."

We shake hands in the Zmaj way, clasping each other's arms at the elbow, then part ways. I stop and take the shoes off before heading to the room they've given us to use. My chest feels empty as I get closer. Will he be there? What do I say?

I've avoided thinking about this all day by focusing on work. Now that it's here, I want to run away. There's no excuse for the way he acted. This is why I can't commit to him. The jealousy of a Zmaj male. I wasn't doing anything, and he lost it. If I hadn't stopped him I think he might have killed Arawn.

"Lana," Olivia calls out.

I walk over to where the curvy red-head is working with the other women. "What's up?"

Her and several others are putting supplies into packs. It looks like they're preparing to travel.

"No clue," she says, wiping sweat from her brow. "One of the dragon-men showed us how to pack these bags with supplies. Made motions until we figured out what he wanted."

"Oh," I say, looking around for one of the Zmaj.

"We were all hoping you knew what's going on," she says.

One of the Zmaj hunters that brought us here is standing a ways off, doing something to his weapons so I walk over.

"Bashir," I say, approaching.

He looks over his shoulder at me then returns his attention to his spear. "Yes?"

"What's going on?"

"The Commander has decided," he says, as if that answers my question.

"Decided? Decided what?"

"We'll harvest epis, it's what you wanted isn't it?" he asks, his voice tight and angry.

"Yes, we need it," I answer, confused at his anger.

"Need it," he spits the words.

"Yes, don't you?"

"Epis is the old ways," he says, turning to face me. "We've been cleansed of it."

Taking a step back I try to meet his glare. Anger pulses from him like warmth from a fire.

"I don't understand," I say. "I thought everyone on Tajss needed epis."

"Only the weak," he says, shaking his head.

I don't understand what he's talking about. The epis changes you at a structural level, making you dependent on it. The Zmaj don't need it often, unlike humans, but they're adjusted to it through generations of exposure. They still need it though. All the Zmaj in Drakonov take it.

"Okay," I say, unwilling to experience more of his anger.

"It doesn't matter," he says. "We will do as the Commander orders. You need it, we'll get it for you."

"Thank you," I say hesitantly, trying to not provoke him further.

He nods then walks off, ending our conversation, so I go back over to Olivia. Several of the women have stopped their work and moved over to see what I have to say.

"They will get epis for us," I say.

"Epis? You mean the magic plant that makes this place

bearable?" a woman named Penelope asks, a hint of laughter in her voice.

She's a pretty girl, extremely tall and thin to the point of being almost gaunt with short, blond hair and gorgeous emerald eyes that flash with sharp intelligence.

"Well it's not magical," I counter. I told them about epis when we all first met but I don't think they believed me. Epis is life on Tajss.

"I'll do anything if it helps with this heat!" Delilah says.

"It does," I say.

"Does it really? You look like shit," Penelope asks.

"I told you, once you take it, you have to take it regularly," I say, adjusting my hair and wiping sweat from my brow.

"Yeah, it's addictive, great," someone says, but I don't see who.

"Okay, well, I need to go," I say, adjusting the shoes on my back as I turn away.

"Lana," Penelope says.

"Yeah?" I ask, not looking back.

"Thank you," she says, then her hand is on my shoulder.

"For what?" I ask, confusion filling me as I turn.

"Helping," she says. "I know, we're not being nice. I'm sorry. I feel like shit, we all do. It's not making us the best people and you're only trying to help. If it wasn't for you we'd still be trying to figure out if the Zmaj were planning to eat us. So thank you."

Tears fill my eyes as my chest constricts. My throat is too tight for words so I nod, smiling. She pulls me into an embrace which I return, grateful. Breaking apart she pats me on the back and I turn and leave.

Facing Astarot seems easier now, though I'm still angry with him I understand. I think anyway. When I enter the room the Tribe gave us I expect to see him waiting for me but it's empty. My stomach drops. Where is he? The suns are setting and the valley of the Tribe isn't large, there aren't many places he could be.

I sit down on the furs that serve as our bed, pull out a piece of meat and lean my back against the wall to eat. The sun's final rays recede, being chased out the cave opening by shadows as night falls.

Alone, I wait until I nod off. A cold fear invades my restless sleep. What if something happened to him? Where is he?

21

ASTAROT

*S*tupid, I admonish myself again. *Losing control like a child throwing a tantrum.*

She is not mine. No matter we have mated, she isn't committed to me. I have of her only what she gives. I don't control her and if she chooses another, then that is my fate.

Crouching low, I run across the sands making my way by smell and instinct. It's not long before I hear the whisper of sismis wings on the air and I know I'm getting closer to my destination. If I'm to lead an expedition for epis, which I will with or without the Tribe, I need to first know where I'm going. Also, I need sismis claws to finish the salve I was teaching Lana to make. So, rather than face her, I'm hunting.

What would I say? Sorry doesn't make it right. I lost control to my bijass. I had no right to do that, to treat her that way, or to do that to Arawn. I'm better than that, not some animal running on instinct. The Tribe has their edicts; they live together without tearing each other apart. As their guest, and as a representative of what we've created for ourselves in Drakonov, I have disgraced myself.

Lana's face swims before my vision. I can't unsee the

disappointment, hurt, and disbelief. I've failed her and I don't know how to fix it.

Shaking my head to clear it, I spot what I'm looking for in the distance. A blackness against the smooth sand of Tajss. Catching my breath there's a flutter of wings and then motion. A clutch of sismis fly out of the black spot taking to the air, screeching their hunting cry.

A cave, just what I wanted. I wait until the clutch has flown off in search of prey then make my way forward. I have to focus on the moment, pushing aside regret and other concerns. It's impossible to do. Lana is always in my thoughts. I get echoes of the sick feeling in my gut when she turned her back, refusing to even look at me.

Closing the distance to the cave, I swallow hard to push it down. Struggling with the nausea and the distractions I'm at the opening before I realize it. Deep breaths, center myself. I can win her back, I have to, life without her is no life at all.

Stopping by the entrance I listen. The soft, rustling sound of leather drifts out of the opening accented by faint whistles. There are more sismis there as I expected. A colony never hunts all at the same time. Some remain behind always to protect the young and guard their adopted home.

Sliding into the hole I lower myself down. The drop is just more than I can reach with my arms fully stretched out. Spreading my wings, I drift down and land in a three point crouch. I hold the position, making sure I didn't create a disturbance. Satisfied, I slide my lochaber off my back then scout out the ceiling. The sismis cling to it, chattering one to another. They nest deeper in the cavern, an old tunnel formed by the passage of a zemlja. Deep into it I see the telltale blue glow of epis. That will be for later, going that deep into the tunnel alone is foolish. I don't have a death wish.

The stronger sismis are deeper. I want one on the edge. Creeping forward until I'm right below one, I pause. No alarm is being raised so I grip my lochaber, spot my target over my head, then in a single swift motion rise and drive the point up and into the large sismis overhead.

It squeaks once then nothing. I drop, the sismis coming down with me attached to my lochaber. As quietly as I can I harvest its claws. The meat of a sismis is foul and useless. The only value of them for a hunter is their claws. Placing them in my pouch, I return to the opening. Leaping and using my wings I grab the edge of the cave then pull myself over the edge.

Lying on the warm sand I stare up at the swirling blackness overhead. The milky white streak of our galaxy is in full view tonight. Twinkling lights sparkle and I wonder if there is still other life out there. The Devastation didn't just affect Tajss; it destroyed this galaxy. The war for epis escalated until there was nothing but a handful of us left. I can only imagine the other planets fared no better or we would have seen them in the years since.

Lana came from beyond our galaxy. Somewhere far, far away. So far that generations of her kind lived and died on the ship while they traveled out in hopes of a new home. What must her home have been like that they would leave it for a home they would never see?

There is no time for considerations. Lana will have missed me by now, at least I hope. The bijass wants her to miss me. It wants to be right for what I did but that's not rational, so I push that feeling aside. Running across the desert on my own I make good time back to the valley. The guards let me pass with little hassle though it's obvious they're surprised I'm returning this far after sunset.

Slipping into our room, Lana is asleep on the mat. She didn't dress for bed or cover up. She must have fallen asleep waiting for me to come in. Running a hand over my face a heavy feeling falls over me. She's beautiful. Her face peaceful in sleep. Kneeling next to her I brush a hair out of her face. She stirs, her eyelids fluttering open.

"Astarot?" she asks sleepily.

"Yes, love," I say, letting the truth be in my words before I think about it.

She stirs, stretching, then sits up. She blinks several times looking at me then rage contorts her delicate features.

"You son of a bitch!" she yells. "How could you disappear like that? Do you know how worried I was? After what you did!"

Heat flushes my body. Shaking my head, I hold my hands up. "Lana," I start but then don't know what to say.

She sobs, tears streaming down her face, then drops back down scooting away until her back is against the wall. She pulls her legs up wrapping her arms around them.

"I thought you were gone," she says without looking up.

A sharp stab into my chest takes my breath. Her worry is palpable, I didn't think of that. Moving to a sitting position, I stare at the floor between us. There isn't a lot of space in our room, we're a few feet apart, but it feels like we're miles away from each other. It's my fault, I created this rift when I lost control.

"I'm sorry," I say, knowing it isn't enough.

She takes a deep, shaky breath before wiping the tears from her cheeks. When she looks up at me her eyes and cheeks are puffy, but she isn't crying any longer.

"Where were you?"

"I got sismis claws," I say, digging them out of my pouch and holding them out in my hand.

She stares at them in disbelief. "You went without me?"

Another stab into my hearts causes them to skip a beat. The pain in her voice is worse than her anger.

"I did it for you," I say, trying to make this right.

She shakes her head side to side. It's not enough, I know it's not.

"I wanted to learn," she says, staring at the yellow-ish claws in the palm of my hand.

"I'll teach you," I say. "If you'll have me."

She looks up from my palm, biting her lower lip. In a sudden burst of motion she flies across the space between us, her arms wrapping around my neck as she hits me in the chest.

"I thought I'd lost you," she sobs into my shoulder.

Wrapping my arms around her, holding her tight against me, nothing else matters. Everything pushes aside in her presence, her in my arms makes the world right. My cock stiffens, her closeness makes it jump in my pants. I'm happy to just hold her but she rises from my shoulder, smiling despite fresh tears on her face, then we're mating with our mouths.

Her lips on mine push my doubts further aside. The only thing I've feared in my life is losing her. She's brought me from resigned and ready to die alone to wanting to live. I want to live for her and because of her.

She grabs my hard cock through my pants and strokes. Her tongue drives into my mouth like an invading army. Groaning as she grips my dick, my eyes roll up into my head. Her soft breasts press into my chest causing an over-whelming amount of sensations.

Laying her down on the furs I work her pants until they give way and slide off of her beautiful legs. She smells sweet, delicate, I long to consume her. Fumbling the way through our clothing until at last my hard cock is at her opening.

We don't stop kissing as I slide into her warmth.

"Take me," she moans.

I drive into her but I can't hold back. The tightness in my core is too much, my need for her overtakes me and I lose control. My cock explodes my seed into her. Pumping her full of my love I let it go, not trying to hold back. Once my prime penis has expended itself, my second descends from inside my tail, hard and ready. Knowing she hasn't yet reached her own climax, I drive straight into her.

"OH!" she gasps in surprise, her eyes widening.

She bites her lower lip and I hesitate, worried I might have hurt her, but then she nods. My desire is unsatisfied, so I take her. Pulling out until just the tip is in her warm, sweet tunnel then I drive in hard until our hips stop my forward thrust. She gasps and moans.

I don't stop. Thrusting in and out, focusing on her. Each move I make that causes her to gasp I repeat. Driving in, I grind my hips and she cries out my name. I keep doing it until she's clawing at my back. When her back arches up and her hips rise to meet mine, I know she's close.

Pushing her to her limits, I drive in again. Forcing her body to mold to mine. I take her neck in my hands and support her as her body spasms, then she arches as her eyes roll up into her head. I hold my position. The muscles of her body spasm then the contractions hit her pussy and I'm over the edge again too.

Her pussy pulses on my cock, milking it. It feels so good all I can do is hiss in pleasure. She takes me for all I'm worth and I give her all I have.

At last our orgasms pass and we collapse into each other.

"I'm sorry," I whisper in her ear.

She's clinging to me, fingertips tracing along my shoulders. She nods beneath me then kisses along my cheekbone.

"It's fine," she says. "I'm sorry I overreacted."

Cuddling together I pull a blanket over us and we drift off to sleep in each other's arms. Morning will come soon.

I'm almost asleep when Lana cries out, sitting up in bed and grabbing her head.

LANA

"*A*gh!" I bite my lip, trying to keep from crying out anymore.

My head is exploding. The pounding spiked and now it feels like something is trying to hammer its way out through my eyes.

"Lana?" Astarot asks, wrapping his arms around me.

"Nothing," I say, gritting my teeth. "My head. It's just the epis withdrawals."

He lets go of me. I can't open my eyes to see what he's doing, even the dim candlelight is making the pain in my head worse. It isn't long before something presses to my lips and I jerk back.

"Eat it," Astarot urges.

"What is it?" I ask.

"Guster meat, it'll help," he says.

I take the meat and chew, though every motion of my jaw makes my head feel worse. Slowly the pain recedes back to the normal pounding.

"It will be better soon," I say, lying back down.

"Not if they don't agree to go with me to get epis," he says.

"I can do it on my own. I'll leave tomorrow, should be back by tomorrow night. There's a cave not far from here."

"You don't have to do that, they're going to send out a team," I say.

"They are? When did that happen?"

"I don't know," I tell him. "When I was on my way here last night, I saw the women were packing bags. When I asked about it I found out they're prepping supplies for an expedition."

"Good!" he says. "This is good. We'll get you the epis soon."

"Not just you, I'm going," I say.

"Lana, you're hurting, you can't."

"I can and I damn well will," I tell him.

His turmoil is palpable in the room. He lies down behind me, spooning in close, and while I'm waiting for him to argue with me, I fall asleep.

RAGNAR STARES AT ME THEN DOWN AT MY SHOES THEN BACK UP at me. He arches one eye then shakes his head and walks into the desert. I follow, doing my best to not give a damn what he or anyone else thinks. The shoes work and that's all that matters.

Astarot walks next to me, Ragnar is in the lead with Bashir. Melchior and two more Zmaj I don't know bring up the rear. As we walk out of the valley, a voice calls out from behind us.

"Astarot," Padraig yells.

Padraig has the deepest voice I've ever heard a Zmaj have, it's booming, and echoes off of the valley walls drifting out to us. The entire party stops, turning to see what the commotion is. Padraig runs out of the valley carrying something. He comes up to Astarot and thrusts the long thing into his hands.

"Edicts are edicts," he says, then turns and walks back into the valley.

Astarot looks down at the object in his hands. I move around him to get a good look. It's a spear, but not just a spear. It's a nice one. Nicer than the ones the other hunters carry with them. It's not as long as theirs, a foot and a half shorter at least.

Astarot inspects it and then whirls it in the air. It makes a whistling sound as he spins it in front of him then up over his head then brings it down and thrusts it forward into an imaginary enemy. The other hunters watch with interest as do I. Satisfied, he nods then turns and holds it out towards me.

Looking from the spear to him in confusion I arch an eyebrow. As I realize what he's doing butterflies dance in my stomach. Swallowing hard to force moisture back into my mouth I struggle to not cry.

"Really?" I ask.

"You've earned it," he says. "A real weapon, you're ready for it."

Everyone is watching as I take the spear. I whirl it, similar to what Astarot just did, then thrust. The weight of it is perfect. It fits in my hand like it was custom made for me. The other hunters hiss and slam their tails against the sand in approval. Facing them, my grin spreading from ear to ear, I give them a half bow then pull out my staff and replace it with the spear.

Pride makes me feel like my chest is swelling to bursting. We resume our journey and as we do, I take Astarot's hand and walk with him. I'm a hunter.

We walk for a couple of hours before Astarot points.

Squinting my eyes I can make out a dark shadow in the ground ahead. Everyone circles around Astarot who kneels.

"When I was there two days ago I saw the glow of epis," he says. "The cave is full of sismis so I didn't go farther in. There could be other predators there. It's a drop, we'll lower Lana down."

"How old did the tunnel look?" Ragnar asks.

"Not old," Astarot says.

Ragnar shakes his head side to side making a whistling sound crossed with a hiss.

"Why does that matter?" I ask.

"An older tunnel means that zemlja that made it is less likely to still be in the area," Rashir answers.

"Oh," I say, thinking about that.

That's what makes gathering epis so dangerous. The zemlja are the top tier predators on the planet. The way I understand it there is nothing higher on the food chain outside a group of Zmaj hunters. Though Ladon killed one on his own, even he says it was a young one and it almost killed him.

Astarot sketches out a plan of attack in the sand. The other hunters weigh in with their thoughts. It isn't but a few minutes before we have a plan and we're heading to the cave. Taking out guster meat, I chew it as I walk. The epis infused meat keeps the shakes at bay and eases the pounding in my head.

"Ragnar, you go first," Astarot says after we reach the cave.

Ragnar drops into the black hole like it's nothing. Looking over the edge I see him land in a crouch with his spear at the ready. He turns a circle, remaining in the crouch then makes a hand signal before he moves to the side. The other hunters drop in one at a time leaving Astarot and I for last.

"I know what you'll say," he says. "But would you stay up here?"

"No way," I answer him.

I hang my feet over the edge of the cave then Astarot takes my hands and lowers me down. The hunters down below grab my legs and lower me to the floor.

My eyes take a moment to adjust to the dimness. I stumble my way to the side, blinking to clear them. Astarot drops almost silently. At last I can see and take a look around. The outside light creates a pool of bright white on the floor but does little to push back the darkness.

There's a rustling sound followed by a soft chitter that makes my skin crawl. The sound echoes off the cavern walls bouncing back and forth making it hard to identify the source. Cold tendrils stretch out from my stomach as goosebumps form on my skin. Astarot puts an arm around me and I jump at his touch.

"Up," he says, his voice a whisper.

Looking up I see the source of the sound. The ceiling is alive once my eyes adjust I see it's covered with enormous bat-like creatures. Sismis, I realize. Knowing the source of the creepy sound takes the fear out of it. Smiling, I nod.

Ragnar is leading the way deeper into the cave and we all fall into the arranged formation. The size of the zemlja that made this tunnel is beyond imagination. I've seen one up close, and that was terrifying but it would have to be three or four times bigger to make a passage this large. I can't imagine running into one that big.

As we move away from the light of the hole, I realize that there's a faint blue glow ahead of us. It grows brighter the deeper we travel. Looking over my shoulder, the light from the hole appears like an empty spotlight shining down. We've moved several hundred yards away now and I can't see well.

The blue glow keeps it from being complete darkness but doesn't do much for lighting up the area.

Astarot's presence next to me is reassuring. Ragnar stops, holding up a closed fist. Everyone moves forward to find that the tunnel has collapsed. There's a tight passage through forcing us to go one by one. The blue glow coming through the crevasse is bright and cheery, calling us forward.

It's a problem in that one person will be on the other side, alone. If there is something on that side or anything goes wrong we won't be able to help. No one speaks, but it's unnecessary. Ragnar nods and moves into the crevasse.

Half-way through he has to turn sideways and squeeze. The sound of his scales scraping against the rock makes me shudder. When he emerges on the other side, his body blocks off most of the light. He stands still for a long moment during which I don't dare breathe. At last he moves. His hand appears, and he makes a come hither motion, indicating the other side is clear.

The hunters head through one at a time. Astarot motions for me to go ahead of him. Butterflies dance in my stomach as I do. The rock walls close in but I'm much smaller than the men. I don't even have to turn sideways to fit through. At one point the walls almost touch my shoulders but even then there's still room.

Coming out on the other side I gasp. The blue glow is brighter, brilliant and sparkling. Long strands of plants hang from the ceiling down to the floor. A long central vine with glowing leaves about as big as my hand dangle off of it. There are hundreds if not thousands of them and their brilliance is reflected in the standing layer of water that covers the cave bottom. It's beautiful and breath-taking.

Astarot touches my shoulder, reminding me I need to move out of the way so he can get out of the crevasse. I don't take my eyes off the scene as I move to one side. Astarot passes through then Ragnar makes hand motions. There wasn't time for Astarot and I to learn their complicated signal system but we get the gist of it.

Bashir, Melchior, and the other two Zmaj move out and begin the work of harvesting. Ragnar, Astarot, and I stand guard while they do. We move out, forming a circle around the gatherers, staring out into the darkness. I don't know how it is for the others but I can only see a few feet ahead before the darkness covers everything.

Nothing happens as time passes. The gatherers work quickly and efficiently. I watch them work with glances over my shoulder as they lay a large piece of oiled leather down below a vine. Two form a cradle with their hands and lift the third. Reaching as high as he can, he uses a knife to cut the vine. It drops to the cloth and they roll it in the leather, taking great care as they do.

They're on their third vine, which is the number we agreed we'd need since storing epis doesn't work for long, when I hear something. My heart pounds in my chest as I strain my eyes into the darkness. It's more a feeling than sight but I'm sure something is moving in the darkness. I can't spot what or where.

My chest rises and falls as my breathing increases to match my heart rate. Tightening my grip on my spear, I take a step out into the dark, hoping it will allow me to see the threat. Ragnar hisses behind me then something crashes. Whirling around Ragnar is sliding on his back across the floor. A thing is on top of him. It's a huge, lizard looking thing with large humps across its back with sharp spikes sticking out of it. Guster!

Ragnar has his spear held crosswise in front of himself and up in the thing's mouth. It's trying to close its razor teeth filled jaw around it, trying to reach Ragnar's head. The gatherers stumble as Ragnar and the creature slide into them, dropping the plant they cut. He hits the ground with a hard slam, cracking his head.

Raising my spear I step forward, intending to stab the creature on Ragnar but the hair on the back of my neck rises. A hissing sound behind me causes a cold chill down my spine. Spinning on my heel I bring the spear up just in time to drive it into the mouth of another one before it can chomp on me.

"Lana!" Astarot screams.

The guster I stabbed howls, almost like a dog crossed over with a cat in some weird way. Jerking its head side to side I struggle to keep my grip on my spear. I'm pulled along with it, my feet sliding across the tunnel floor. Digging my heels in I try to pull the spear free but I can't find purchase.

More motion around us. There are more of the damn things attacking! Holding on to my spear I'm drug along by the mewling monster. I can't lose my spear. Looking at the angle it's stuck in, an idea occurs. Instead of trying to pull the spear free, in a single forward motion I drive my weight into it, pushing off the ground and up into it.

Blood and goo spew out of the thing's mouth then it screams and falls to the ground with a thump. Bracing my foot against its lower jaw I'm able to jerk my spear free. Wiping gunk from my eyes I turn around. Ragnar is still on the ground, struggling with the first and largest guster that attacked. It must be the bull. I see bloody tears in his arms and chest where the monster has bitten him. Astarot is fending off two others with his lochaber and can't help Ragnar. Bashir and Melchior are trapped in a corner by several other beasts and the gatherers are backing away from yet another one.

I scream, charging the one on top of Ragnar with my spear in front of me. My loud yell distracts it momentarily and it pulls back from Ragnar, but he pushes his spear forward, keeping it in the thing's jaws. It's the opening I need. Adjusting my spear as I run, I drive the point into the thing's eye and into its brain. The creature falls without a sound on top of Ragnar.

Breathing heavily I look for the next threat. Astarot has killed one and is attacking another. The gatherers have gotten their spears out and are holding off the one threatening them. Bashir and Melchior look to have the rest in hand. Ragnar climbs out from under the one we just felled and moves to help the gatherers so I head towards the last one threatening Astarot.

Astarot's lochaber whirls through the air with a whistling sound then connects with the neck of the monster. Blood spurts out, and the creature howls in pain. As one he and I drive our spears into it from both sides and it shudders, then drops to the ground dead. My limbs shake as the threat passes and my heart pounds in my chest.

"That will handle the hunt for this passage," Ragnar calls.

Bashir laughs then the rest of us join in. Ragnar moves to stand in front of me, visibly wounded. Panting from the exertion, I look up at his greater height. He stares down until I'm feeling uncomfortable.

"You saved my life," he says.

"You would have had it, I just helped," I say.

"No," he shakes his head. "I wouldn't. You are a hunter."

My chest tightens until I can't breathe. My heart is pounding double time in my chest, butterflies dance in my stomach, my knees shake as tears form in the corners of my eyes. I can't speak, words won't form. Meeting Astarot's eyes I see something in them, pride.

"Thank you," my voice squeaks when at last I speak.

Ragnar nods holding his hand out. I take his arm, Zmaj style.

"Thank you," he replies.

He lets my arm go then issues orders to harvest the meat before we leave. Astarot comes over and pulls me into a tight embrace.

"I'm so proud," he whispers, making my heart swell again.

He doesn't drag the moment out with so many watching us. We set about doing our part to harvest the kill and prepare to take it back to the Tribe.

23

ASTAROT

*R*osalind *will be furious,* I think, walking through the valley. *We need to go home, soon.*

Lana and I have been discussing this. Now that she has epis she is no longer suffering from withdrawal. We don't have enough to get us home. While I have a good idea of where to go, it's just an idea. I'm sure if I can get close I can get us there.

The other human females have all agreed to take the epis. They haven't balked at being stuck here like some of the humans in Drakonov. They, at least, have accepted that Tajss is their home now. Lana has spent most of the last several days with them. Teaching them basic words, showing them how to use and store the epis. Anything to help them adjust to Zmaj culture.

It's obvious, now that I've had a few days, that several of these Zmaj have already felt the call towards certain of the females. That will play out in time, I'm sure. If I could convince them all to come back to Drakonov with us, we could use the machine to teach them to speak Zmaj in an instant.

Visidion and I have already argued about this many times. He's set on the idea the Tribe belongs here. When last I talked, the Elders were there and Kesselin said something odd before he left the room. He said, 'It's not time, yet.'

I have no idea what that means.

It doesn't matter though. I have to figure out a way to get us back to Drakonov. The other females want to take epis to their friends and family at the other crash site, too. That is easier than trying to get Lana and I back to Drakonov at least. Maybe once Ragnar heals he'll help me do that for them. Lana being able to translate should make it possible to interact with them without causing a panic.

"He's in the back," Ormarr says, as I walk into his cave.

Ormarr is a healer. He has bright eyes and colorful scales that are brighter than most Zmaj, all emblematic of his position in our former society.

"Thanks," I say, walking past him and then through a leather curtain at the back side of the space.

Ragnar is sitting up and extending his wing then pulling it back. He looks up as I enter, frowns, then works his wing again.

"Getting better?" I ask.

"Yes," he answers, sullen. "It's healing too slow."

"You're lucky all you did was tear the tendons," I say.

"What do you want?" he asks, glaring at me.

"I was going to propose an expedition to the humans near here," I say. "Take Lana so she can introduce the Tribe to them. Offer them epis, let them know where their missing females are."

"Why?" he grouses.

"Why not?" I ask. "They're not prisoners, they want to see their friends and families."

Ragnar shakes his head, winces in pain, then sighs.

"Sure, I'll talk with the Commander about it."

"Good," I say. "Do you need anything?"

"No," he says, his brow furrows as he continues working his damaged wing.

"All right, I'll check with-"

A blood-curdling scream cuts me off mid-sentence. Ragnar and I exchange a quick look before he's following me out into the valley. More screams and shouts are followed by the ringing clash of weapons. Chaos grips the valley. A Zmaj runs past me towards the entrance carrying a spear. Two others run towards the rear of the valley.

"What is it!" I yell, grabbing one of the Zmaj as he passes.

"Zzlo," he pants, fear in his eyes.

"No," Ragnar exhales.

Just then I see them. A Zmaj I don't recognize is just ahead but he's not fighting, he's grabbing other Zmaj and pummeling them with his bare fists. The new Zmaj looks wild, he's roaring, wearing only a cloth around his waist. Several Zmaj are closing with him, wielding spears. He grabs a spear as it's thrust towards him, pulling the unfortunate Zmaj in. He grabs the Zmaj, lifts him over his head as if he weighs nothing and throws him into the others.

Behind him are five Zzlo firing their electrical weapons at anything that moves. One of them, in the center of the group, has a long pole with a bulky end that crackles with live electricity. He uses this to poke and prod the crazed Zmaj, controlling him.

"See that?" I ask Ragnar.

"Yeah," he says.

"We have to stop that one," I say.

"Right, let's go," he answers.

As we run towards the invaders, Drosdan, the Commander's Second, bounds up next to me. He's so big as to make me feel like a human next to him. He roars and it echoes off of the walls of the valley. Two of the Zzlo look and point.

They bring their weapons to bear on him. He bounds forward then leaps into the air, his wing spread is so wide it casts a huge shadow across the ground. The Zzlo fire at him and I'm sure some must hit but he lands in the middle of their group, tearing into them.

The one with the stick guiding the crazed Zmaj maneuvers him, turning him towards Drosdan. I don't waste the opportunity. Grabbing the Zzlo from behind, I wrap my arm around his neck and squeeze. He yelps in surprise but I'm able to choke him out despite his struggling.

The crazed Zmaj rushes towards Drosdan, screaming a primal sound. Drosdan is in the middle of the Zzlo. Their weapons are hitting him over and over but he powers through, taking them out one at a time. Other Zmaj join him and the fight is swinging in our favor but the crazed one will ruin it all. Looking around, no one else sees what's about to happen.

I dive forward, spreading my wings to catch what air I can, and tackle the enemy Zmaj. I hit the back of his head with my shoulder and we hit the ground together. Rolling over and over we come to a halt with him on top of me. He screams, throwing his arms wide, puffing out his chest. Vicious scars and open wounds cover his body. He doubles up his fists and slams them against my head.

Pain. White hot explosions rock through me. Coppery blood fills my mouth. I throw my hands up to protect myself. He flails wildly, blows raining down. Kicking up to knock him off of me doesn't work. He rolls with it but never stops hitting me. There is no intelligence to his fighting, only blind attacks. Hitting my arms, chest, and the sides of my head. A blow gets past my guard, hitting my left eye. I feel it swelling and my vision restricts. I'm losing.

Rage rises with the pain. No one beats me. I won't lose. The bijass flows in, trying to take control.

"Astarot!"

Lana's voice.

The blows stop, just for an instant. He's turning his attention to her. I know it, she's too brave. She'll try to save me. No, I have to save her.

Red clouds my vision as the bijass takes over but as I give over to it I see her. The look on her face when I lost control. No, rage isn't the answer.

Edicts. Edicts are life. Edicts bring us together.

"Don't kill him!" Ragnar yells.

The mantra, I repeat it, and my mind clears. He's distracted, looking at Lana, so I take the opportunity before me. A hard right under his chin and his head cracks back, blood flying. My tail comes up, slamming into him again. His eyes widen in surprise as he cries out in pain. Instead of fighting more, he curls into a ball.

Rising I stand over him, he doesn't move, but whimpers. Ragnar appears beside me then kneels next to the enemy Zmaj, but he jerks away as Ragnar reaches for him.

"No," Ragnar says, his voice soft, shaking his head.

"What is it?" I ask.

"Ryuth, what have they done?" he asks the crazed one.

"Ragnar, you know him?" I ask.

He looks over his shoulder and nods. "This is my brother."

A sickness grips my stomach looking at the broken shell of a Zmaj warrior. One who has given in to the bijass.

"I'm sorry," I say.

Ragnar's face hardens. Looking out at the Zzlo, he grips his spear tighter.

"Make them pay," he hisses, charging into the fight.

Ragnar races at the group of Zzlo, dodging left and right, avoiding their gunfire. Reaching the first one he swings his spear around, bringing the butt hard against the Zzlo's head and spinning him around. He fights with unmatched rage.

Between Ragnar's rage and Drosdan's size, the fight with the Zzlo turns in our favor. Several of them are down but the remaining few are retreating out of the valley. It's not a full route, they're maintaining discipline, firing as they back out.

Several Zmaj take hits. A Zmaj leaps from the top of the valley, hitting a Zzlo and tumbling him out of the fight. There are four remaining slavers. They're exiting the entrance to the valley with a mob of Zmaj chasing them led by Ragnar. They have to have a transport. If I can get that, then I have a way to get us back to Drakonov.

I run. They're holding a position at the opening where it's small enough to keep the Zmaj from flanking them. Seeing this, I change directions and run up a ramp on the walls to the second level of caves. Reaching the top of it I leap and grab the edge of the valley top. Scrambling over I resume running.

Swinging wide to avoid possible guards, I come around to the entrance to the valley. The transport is sitting there not far at all. The Zzlo have all their attention on the defense they're mounting and don't notice me running for their transport. I'm almost there when the sizzle of electricity whizzes past, just in front of me. They've noticed me.

Pouring everything I've got into my run, I move faster, spreading my wings and leaping every other step. My foot lands on the metal ramp with a clang. Electric bolts hit the transport on either side. Ducking, I run inside. Having been captive in one of these before, I'm familiar with the layout.

Going through the door that leads to the front there's a door on the wall. Ripping it open, inside is one of their lightning weapons. I grab it and at the same time I hear footsteps on the metal ramp. I turn and fire without looking. The Zzlo takes the hit in the face, flying backwards and slamming to the ground.

Outside an engine whines. Running out and waving the

gun around, I see another Zzlo has mounted some kind of smaller machine. It's long and thin with a seat on top. He looks over his shoulder then does something and the machine jumps into motion. Firing at his retreating form I don't even come close to hitting him.

His form fades away in the distance. The Zzlo will be back with reinforcements.

24

LANA

"There is no choice!" Astarot says, raising his voice over the clamor.

The Tribe has gathered in the open space of the valley before the Commander's cave. My fellow human women huddle together, staying close. I'm doing my best to translate for them but it's hard to keep up. The conversation is fast and furious.

Ragnar and Astarot are face to face. The Commander and the two Elders watch them argue. Beside Visidion stands Drosdan, his Second, with his massive arms crossed over his chest. The crowd of Zmaj are shouting back and forth as a split forms among them. Some favoring Astarot's plan, while others are on Ragnar's side.

Chewing on my lower lip I watch them argue. Astarot is right, the Tribe cannot stay here. The pirates know they're here and they will be back. They're slavers, how could they not return with enough force to capture everyone here? And what they did to that poor Zmaj that lead the attack!

A cold grip squeezes my heart thinking about him, Ryuth. Ragnar, his brother, told us his name. Astarot may have beaten Ryuth but the signs of their fight are all over Astarot's face. It was a close fight. Ormarr has that one restrained. He says it will take time but he should be able to nurse him back to health. The healer said nothing about his sanity returning.

"This is the Tribe's home," Ragnar says. "I will not give it over."

"You don't have a choice!" Astarot says, continuing the argument.

They've been at it for an hour at least. The Commander and Elders haven't said a word, only watched as the two men argue and the Tribe splits almost even between their opposing views.

"We do, we fight!" Ragnar says and his side of the group cheers, brandishing their spears.

"Right," Astarot sighs, shaking his head. He turns, looking at me and the women standing with me. "What about them?"

The cheers trail off as the Zmaj look at each other then at us.

"What do you mean?" Ragnar asks. "We protect them! We fight for them."

Astarot nods, slow and thoughtful. "Sure," he says. "You'll fight. You might win, sometimes. How many were hurt this time? And the next time? How many the time after that? How long before there are so many of them you not only lose, they take your females? What then?"

I translate for the women behind me.

"I'm not any alien dragon-man's female," Delilah says, snapping her fingers. "They best be thinking again!"

"Do they mean we're never going free?" Olivia asks.

The other women speak over each other in a rising panic. Great, not what I intended. My mom, Bailey, steps out of the crowd and stands next to me. The other girls continue feeding each other's rising panic until she puts two fingers in her mouth and rips out a whistle that so loud it echoes off the stone walls of the valley. Silence falls not only over the girls but all the Zmaj behind us, too.

"Listen," Bailey says. "These men have been good to us and you're all acting like brats. This planet sucks, we know, and our survival is far from assured. I'm not saying you all need to pick a mate but working together improves not only our survival but theirs too."

"Yeah but-" Delilah says.

"No buts," Bailey cuts her off. "We have to face some hard truths. Lana says she and the other survivors are living in what was once a great city. Now I don't know about you but that sounds a lot better than the wreck of our ship we're calling home."

Muttered agreement from the girls. All the Zmaj are staring, their arguments halted.

"Care to translate?" Astarot asks.

"Sure," I say, and tell them what Bailey said.

"I like it," Penelope says. "We should go there. A dome and a real room to call home? I'm in."

Kesselin is whispering to the Commander who then taps his staff three times pulling everyone's attention. "Astarot is right," he says.

I swear you could hear a pin drop, the silence is so complete. I translate for the humans, speaking softly and they nod, feeling the solemnity of the moment. No one says anything more, they all just leave. Soon I'm standing alone with Astarot and Ragnar.

"You got your way," Ragnar grouses, still upset.

"I only want to help," Astarot says.

"We'll see," Ragnar says, turning and walking away.

Alone, we stare at each other and then warmth forms in my core, spreading throughout. The slight breeze blowing through the valley touches my skin, raising goosebumps as butterflies dance in my stomach. An empty ache follows and looking at him I know it's time.

"Astarot," I say, breathless, my pulse racing.

"Yes?" he asks, staring into my eyes.

I'm falling into those violet pools.

"I love you," the words fall off my tongue unbidden, carrying more than three simple words ever could.

Time freezes, the world is just the two of us. Profound words, spoken in a moment of naked truth, exposing my soul. His strong arms wrap around me, protecting, lifting me off my feet and then our lips crash together in a joining. Time resumes as he whirls me, turning a circle.

When our lips part he's laughing. Tears run down my face as I wrap my legs around his waist. He kisses me again, his eyes sparkle with delight. As we kiss, it fills the emptiness inside me with him. Distant clapping invades the moment and I realize that we're not alone. Astarot sets me back on the ground and I turn to see we've attracted a crowd, including my mom.

"I love you, with all that I am," Astarot says, keeping an arm around me.

"Mom!" I exclaim, my voice cracking with unrestrained emotions.

She runs forward and wraps her arms around both of us.

"I'm so happy for you," she says.

"NERVOUS?" MOM ASKS.

"Shouldn't I be?" I ask back, laughing to keep myself from exploding.

"You look amazing!" Penelope exclaims.

"I do?" There are no mirrors here, makes it hard to get an outside perspective.

"I told you so already," Mom says.

"I know, but you're biased," I grin.

I'm wearing a finely stitched, exquisitely soft, bleached leather dress. Arawn provided the materials and apparently Astrid is really good at sewing. Somehow, they pulled together a simply beautiful dress. Olivia found something like charcoal and she's used it to line my eyes, it's the best we've got.

Today I'm committing to Astarot. I've never heard about the ceremony but the Commander insisted he perform it before we leave. He wants the honor himself he says. A way of thanking us for coming in their time of need.

Emotions so strong grip me I can't tell if I will cry or explode. I do my best to control them, laughing and giggling to let the pressure out. A dozen hugs later and I'm lead outside. My mom walks beside me and the other women fall in behind, making a train.

We walk down the ramp from the second tier room we prepped in. The Zmaj males line the walls of the valley. When we reach the bottom of the stone ramp, they step forward as one. It makes a sharp, stomping sound as they do. My heart pounds in my chest as my pulse races faster than a ship breaking gravity.

Astarot is standing at the end of the line of men, all of them with their spears angled in forming a tunnel for me to walk. As I approach they pull their spears back. Blinking to keep the tears at bay I walk slow, savoring each moment. There is an unreality to the world.

None of the other girls back home had anything like this. They said they were together, and that was it. There aren't this many Zmaj back at Drakonov so ceremony isn't a big deal. I'm light-headed, dizziness spinning around my head like I'm circling and about to fall. I can feel my breathing increase until I'm sure I'll hyperventilate.

Locking eyes with Astarot the spinning stops. He's my rock. His beautiful face, those stunning eyes, his strong broad shoulders, bulging arms ready to carry me through anything. When he smiles, I know he loves me. I'm important to him.

He takes my hands in his and I look up. We stare at each other, silent, letting the crowd see us. The Commander lays his hands on ours, gripping them. His cool hands are almost cold, despite the heat. A bead of sweat runs down my brow, my heart is doing double time beats. This is it.

"Astarot," the Commander says. "Your heart has yearned and been answered. Is this the female you would share water with?"

"It is," Astarot says, his voice strong and certain.

"Lana, your heart has answered the call. Is this the male you would share water with?"

"It is," I answer, no hesitation.

The Commander holds his hands on ours a moment longer then steps back. Drosdan moves forward. He's carrying a barrel so big that his arms can barely wrap around it. Despite his massive size it's obvious he's straining. It looks like a job for two or three but Drosdan is that way.

He sets the barrel down with a grunt. Sand flies up as it drops the last few inches to the ground. Rising and moving to the side the Commander comes back up. He takes the lid off of the barrel. Inside is water, cold, cool, refreshing water. An excessive amount.

"Water brings life," the Commander says. "In sharing water, you commit one to another and both to all of us. Our future rests on you."

He places his cupped hands in the barrel then moves over to Astarot and pours water over his head. Stepping back to the barrel he gets another handful of water then pours it over my head. I gasp as the cold liquid drips down my face and runs down my spine. Then he steps back. Astarot steps to the barrel, cups his hands and draws water, and turns.

"I give you my water," he says, pouring water over my head.

Shivering as it runs down my spine, I lift my head up and accept his gift. He embraces me, lifting me off my feet, and then his lips are on mine. Applause and cheers break out around us but its distant. There is only the two of us, here together. Committed one to another.

Astarot doesn't set me down, carrying me through the cheering, chanting crowd. His mouth devours me as we walk. My lips, neck, cheeks, kissing and nibbling. In moments the walls of our space muffle the sounds of the crowd. He sets me down on the furs then steps back, looking me up and down.

"You're beautiful," he exhales, his hard cock tenting out his trousers.

My cheeks flush hot and I look down at the ground.

"Thank you," I mutter.

"Lana, I love you. The first moment I saw you, I knew you were my treasure. You're strong, beautiful, and amazing. Allow me to worship you."

I want to respond but he's too fast. Moving, he grabs my dress and pulls it over my head in a single motion, tossing it aside. His hands roam up my legs and sides then he's kissing his way down across my breasts. Dragging his tongue across my stomach I shudder as he kisses still lower.

Is he? I hardly have the thought before he's there.

His rough, warm tongue caresses my soft folds. I gasp in surprise, he's never done this for me. His rough tongue laps from the bottom of my opening to the top, staying outside my soft folds. His firm grip on my thighs is controlling, dominating in a way that makes me wet.

"Mmm," I moan, as he laps my wet slit.

His tongue works like magic, driving into me, exploring. Electric sensations explode, racing through my body. I grab my tits, pulling at the nipples while his tongue works up and down, grazing my clit with each up stroke. He sucks my swollen lips and I pinch my nipples rolling them in my fingers.

I cry out my pleasure as he sucks then he slides a finger in below his tongue, filling me. I'm moaning and squirming under his touch. His finger slides in slowly while his tongue resumes licking my folds. His exploration is too much. My hips buck up, driving his finger in deep.

He drags his tongue up and down faster, pressing into my clit each time, winding me tighter. The pressure in my core is building. I'm panting and moaning in time with my pounding heart. Breath is short gasps of pleasure. His finger is driving in and out of my pussy. His tongue, that expert touch, digging through my folds until he finds my hard nub and circles it with the tip.

"Ahh!" I cry out, pleasure gripping me tight.

He presses in harder, smashing his tongue against my clit then moving up and down while keeping a hard pressure on it. His finger drives deep. He moves his head side to side, the roughness of his tongue pulling my clitoris with his motion and I lose it.

"Ah, ah, ah! Oh!" I cry out, my back arching, my toes curling, my thighs clamping against his head.

My body shudders and spasms as the orgasm rips through me like fire through dry brush. Gone is all sense, there is only pleasure.

Awareness returns in a slow, steady pace. Muscles unlock until I fall back against the soft furs, panting and exhausted. I've never come so hard before in my life.

He moves up over me then his cock is at my opening. I'm wet, ready, and oh so relaxed. His massive girth slides in and in moments I'm building towards a fresh orgasm. He grunts as I take his cock until he's panting too. We thrust into each other consummating the ceremony.

He spills his seed into me and I take it until he and I become us. We become one in our joining, melding our bodies together.

He collapses on top of me. The weight of him is comforting as his cock softens inside. We kiss, soft, gentle kisses that taste even sweeter because of our commitment to each other. Time passes before he pulls out. His second cock is hard but we're both tired, so instead of more I lie on my side and we cuddle up together.

Tomorrow we board our liberated transport. Rosalind is in for the shock of her life. Everyone is! First, we'll go to the second crash site, then home to Drakonov. I'm sure they'll get over any upset about us being gone far longer than planned. Thinking about the look on my friends' faces when I return, not only committed to Astarot, but with an entire entourage of new Zmaj and more humans makes me happy.

I may not have belonged on the generation ship but I've found my place on Tajss. A whole new world is opening before us.

Again. I can't wait to share it with them.

THE END

ABOUT THE AUTHOR

USA Today Bestselling Author of fantasy and scifi romance, Miranda Martin's books feature larger than life heroes with out-of-this-world anatomy and smart heroines destined to save the world. As a little girl she would sneak off with her nose in a book, dreaming of magical realms. Today she brings those fantasies to life and adores every fan who chooses to live in them for a while.

She was born and raised in southern Virginia, but as a veteran she's traveled to places like Korea, Hawaii and good 'ole Texas. Now she's settled in Kansas, the heart of America, with her husband and daughters. Her favorite animals are dragons, unicorns and cats. If she's not writing, you can still find her tucked away somewhere with a warm blanket and her nose in a book.

Get in touch!
mirandamartinromance.com
miranda@mirandamartinromance.com

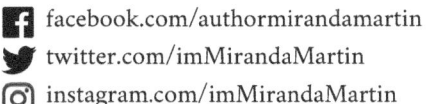

facebook.com/authormirandamartin
twitter.com/imMirandaMartin
instagram.com/imMirandaMartin

FULL COPYRIGHT